Hell, he didn't even know her real name, but that didn't matter. The only thing that mattered to him was he wanted her and he wanted her bad. More than he could recall ever wanting a woman before, and that was definitely a new experience for him.

He led Red into the elevator and no sooner had the door swooshed close behind them, he crushed her to him, had her against the wall, and his mouth came charging down. He heard her purse drop seconds before she wrapped her arms around his neck and parted her lips to return his blazing kiss. He actually felt every part of him on fire and blood was pumping through his veins like crazy.

He loved her taste and deepened the kiss. His tongue skillfully moved from one side of her mouth to the other, exploring, tasting, stirring sensations he wanted her to feel. Some primitive force was taking over his senses, somehow convincing him that she would be different than all his other one-nighters. For the life of him, he couldn't understand or accept that nonsense. But still, a part of him was helpless to control the raging desire fueling within him.

Books by Brenda Jackson

Harlequin Kimani Romance

BRENDA JACKSON

is a die "heart" romantic who married her childhood sweetheart and still proudly wears the "going steady" ring he gave her when she was fifteen. Because she's always believed in the power of love, Brenda's stories always have happy endings. In her real-life love story, Brenda and her husband of thirty-nine years live in Jacksonville, Florida, and have two sons.

A *New York Times* and *USA TODAY* bestselling author of over ninety romance titles, Brenda is a retiree from a major insurance company and now divides her time between family, writing and traveling with Gerald. You may write Brenda at P.O. Box 28267, Jacksonville, Florida 32226; email her at AuthorBrendaJackson@gmail.com or visit her website at www.brendajackson.net.

BRENDA JACKSON

BACHELOR UNCLAIMED

◆ HARLEQUIN® KIMANI™ ROMANCE

Recycling programs
for this product may
not exist in your area.

ISBN-13: 978-0-373-86292-4

BACHELOR UNCLAIMED

Printed in U.S.A.

Dear Reader,

Please envision six men who, for various reasons, are members of the Bachelor in Demand Club, and are determined to stay single for as long as they can. With each book I write in this series, I am having fun making each man open their hearts to love when the right woman comes along.

Bachelor Unclaimed's hero is Winston Coltrane and his leading lady is Ainsley St. James. Winston is a dedicated, hard-working marine biologist who knows when he needs play time. When he meets Ainsley while she is vacationing in Hilton Head, he is ready for the fun to begin. They soon discover too much fun can lead to memories you can't shake no matter how much you try. The big question is whether Winston and Ainsley can have their fun and keep their hearts intact.

I hope all of you enjoy reading Winston and Ainsley's story.

Happy reading!

Brenda Jackson

To the love of my life, Gerald Jackson, Sr.

To the ladies of Diva Dayz 2012.
I enjoyed the week of friendship and sisterhood
during our time in Savannah and Hilton Head.

Special thanks to author Beverly Jenkins
for her history lesson on Robert Small.

To the Michelville Preservation Society
for providing tours and lectures that were rich in
Hilton Head Island and Gullah history and heritage.

He hath made every thing beautiful in his time.
—*Ecclesiastes* 3:11

Chapter 1

"So, what brings you across the Port Royal Sound, Win?"

Winston Coltrane sat across the counter from his childhood friend, Grady Parker, who moonlighted as a bartender at the Sparrow, a popular nightclub located within the Regency Resort in Hilton Head. Winston shrugged and asked, "I need a reason?"

Grady chuckled. "Hell, yeah. Even when we were kids it was hard to get you off that damn island."

Winston couldn't help smiling as he took a sip of his Scotch. What Grady said was true. Even leaving Barrett Shores, the ten-thousand-acre barrier island that had been in his family since the end of the Civil War, to attend college hadn't been easy for him. The island had withstood a lot over the years, including several hurricanes and a hostile takeover attempt by a group of developers with plans to transform the island into an exclusive resort community. "Well, I'm here with a room upstairs for the next two nights," he said.

One of those cheesy grins slid onto Grady's face. "Two nights? Must mean you need to get laid pretty bad. I understand. Happens to the best of us."

Grady paused from wiping off the counter to add, "If you thought Sophie was going to take care of your horny needs then I hate to disappoint you. She left New Year's Day for Miami."

A hot liaison with Sophie Causey had been foremost in Winston's mind. He hadn't had a woman in over six months, and he'd counted on those two nights with her. "Who does Sophie know in Miami?"

"Some cousin who's competing in a tennis tournament. She'll be gone for two weeks."

Disappointed, Winston took another sip of his drink. His very casual affair with Sophie worked well for him and for her. After Sophie's divorce three years ago, she'd sworn up and down Main Street that she would never marry again and that her only relationship with men would be for pleasure-sex only. Those had been Winston's sentiments exactly. Any thoughts of settling down with one woman had come to a screeching halt in college when a coed by the name of Caroline Darling had shown him just how deceitful some women could be.

He was about to ask for a refill on his glass of Scotch when something beyond his shoulder made Grady's eyes almost pop out of the sockets. "Hell, if I didn't love my wife so much, I would be all over her. She's hot."

Curious, Winston jerked around his head, nearly getting whiplash in the process. He let out a low whistle as his gaze roamed up and down the woman who'd just walked through the door. His pulse quickened and a breath was released from his lungs in one heated rush. She was more than hot. The woman was in flames.

Her hair, a mass of spiral curls, highlighted her

cinnamon-toned complexion and made every feature of her face striking. His fingers actually itched at the thought of running through those curls on her head.

But what really had his erection throbbing big-time was her outfit—a one-sleeved formfitting red mini dress that showed off every curve of her body. And she definitely had the legs for it in those killer red stilettos.

She had captured the attention of every man in the room, even the musicians who all but stopped playing their instruments to stare at her. But she seemed oblivious to the attention she was getting as she glanced around for an available table.

"Um, do you think Carol would forgive me if I was unfaithful just this one time?" he heard Grady ask. He knew his friend was joking because Grady loved his wife to distraction.

"Carol might forgive you but I won't because I'm going to claim that woman tonight for myself, so don't get any ideas," Winston said.

"Evidently you have a few ideas of your own. You think she'll agree to any of them?" Grady asked him.

"Yes."

He heard Grady chuckle. "You sound pretty damn confident as usual, Win."

The woman crossed the room to an empty table and Winston watched how the hem of her short dress rode up her thighs with every step she took. And when she slid into her chair, that itsy-bitsy dress barely covered those same thighs. He swallowed deeply. And they were luscious brown thighs.

"That's the only way to get anything done," he finally said. "Just watch how things are about to go down."

And going down they would, he thought, already envisioning their hot naked bodies on silken sheets making love nonstop. He took another sip of his drink, licked his lips and then placed the glass on the counter and slowly began moving across the room toward the woman in red.

Ainsley St. James glanced around thinking this was exactly what she needed, especially tonight. She had been in Hilton Head only a couple days and was still trying to replace the angry Ainsley St. James of Claxton, New Jersey, with the I-don't-give-a-royal-damn Ainsley. The same one who'd escaped to this seaside community, to forget that the man who'd defeated her in her bid as mayor of her hometown had been sworn in today, and she hadn't wanted to be anywhere near Claxton.

She could just imagine what kind of inauguration party Luis Higgins was throwing about now. She'd heard the guest list was long and it wouldn't surprise her if the small town of fifteen thousand was going in debt to pay for the new mayor's extravagancies.

Okay, it wasn't meant for her to be mayor of Claxton. She got that…finally. But what she couldn't get past was the nasty campaign Higgins had run, especially the lies he'd fabricated. And even worse was how the good people of Claxton—those who'd vowed to back her until the end—had been gullible enough to believe them.

However, her intention tonight was to put all that to the back of her mind and have some long overdue fun. The concierge at the resort where she was staying for the next two weeks had suggested the Sparrow. The club was crowded but then it was a Friday night. She'd been lucky to find a table, even if it was a small one in the corner.

She watched several couples move toward the dance floor to enjoy the hip-hop sound the live band was blasting out. Tonight she intended to get on that same floor even if she had to dance by herself. She liked dancing, hadn't done it in a while and had quite a few issues to shake, rattle and roll right out of her system.

She took a sip of the water from the glass a waitress had quickly placed on her table before hurrying off to service another customer. At that moment Ainsley wasn't sure what made her tilt her head to look toward the bar but, when she did her breath caught at the dark, intense gaze that snagged hers. Her heart skipped a beat and a warm surge of heat flooded her.

She'd heard of immediate sexual attraction but hadn't believed such a thing existed until now. She sat there, mesmerized as the tall, dark and handsome man appeared to be weaving his way through the crowd toward her.

Her?

Lordy, she mouthed under her breath. She hoped not, because she was definitely not ready for the likes of him. Everything about the man was overwhelming. He had to be every bit of six-three and was wearing a pair of pleated black slacks and a white shirt that was opened at the top and revealed just a smidgen of a hairy chest. Too bad she'd always had a thing for hairy-chested men because now she wondered just how far down his chest that patch went. Then there were his broad muscular shoulders, flat abs, strong arms and powerful long legs. Never had she seen a male so good-looking and fine.

And he was eating up the distance between them in a sensual stride that had shivers inching up her spine. Her gaze moved back to his eyes that were focused solely on her.

She would guess his age at thirty-three or thirty-four. He had chestnut-colored skin, bedroom-brown eyes, a perfectly shaped nose, rugged jaw and an arrogant mouth. That mouth gave her pause and she immediately concluded that he saw her as a conquest with him as the conqueror.

For the first time in all her twenty-six years of life, the

thought of such a thing did not bother her because she could definitely understand any woman lowering her guard a little for the likes of him. The thought of being taken by him, in any shape, form or position, had her stomach fluttering wildly.

Okay, Ainsley St. James, get rid of all those lusty thoughts or you might end up in his bed later. You came here to let your hair down, but, girl, please keep your panties up, she lectured herself. Deciding it was time to get her guard back in place, she squared her shoulders and sat straighter in her chair, wanting to stop him in his tracks.

When he came to a halt in front of her table, she tilted her head and met the intensity of his dark eyes when he simply said, "Hi."

That was it? No pickup line? Just a simple *hi?* She frowned. "Do I know you?"

For a moment he only stood there and smiled at her, and then he leaned down close, his breath warming the skin near her ear when he whispered, "No, not now. But the minute I make love to you, you will."

Chapter 2

Winston was tempted to kiss that shocked look right off the woman's lips but decided he needed to retain his cool. He stared at her knowing it was just a matter of time before she put him in his place, and when she did he would do the same to her. But even with the shock on her face, he'd seen it—that flash of desire that had lit her eyes before he'd come on to her.

"How dare you say something like that to me," she said in a breathless rush.

He slid into the chair across from her. "I dare because I saw the way you were looking at me."

The frown on her face deepened. "I was not looking at you in any particular way."

"I beg to differ," he said, leaning close to her and thinking the shape of her mouth was a total turn-on.

"You can beg all you want, mister."

"Not mister. Winston. And you are?"

"You don't need to know my name."

He shrugged. "That's fine. For now I'll just call you Red. That color looks great on you, by the way."

She rolled her eyes. "Don't exert your efforts since they won't work on me."

"They won't?"

"No."

"I think any effort I invest in you will be well worth it," he said. "May I join you?"

"It seems you already have."

She was right, he had. Was that irritation he heard in her voice or anticipation? Usually he wasn't this forward with a woman, nor as pushy. But there had been this instant connection between them the moment their gazes had met, whether she admitted to it or not.

"So where are you from, Red?"

If he thinks he's getting any information out of me, he's as crazy as he is bold, Ainsley thought, taking another sip of her water. And where was the waitress? She needed that margarita right now. Up close the man was simply gorgeous and each time he spoke she could feel her stomach quivering.

"What makes you think I'm not from here?" she asked, feeling pleasure radiating through her traitorous body. The man had a sexual magnetism that was slowly drawing her in, eroding her resistance. And he smelled so darn good. She was tempted to ask him what cologne he was wearing.

"Lucky guess," he said, reclaiming her attention.

She glanced around for a waitress before returning her gaze to him. When their eyes locked, her pulse rate increased. She swallowed deeply before saying, "I take that to mean you're from Hilton Head."

"No, I'm not."

"Then where are you from?" she inquired, trying to see

if she could decipher his accent. There was enough of a Southern drawl to let her know he was from the South. Possibly Tennessee or Texas.

"I asked you first."

And she had no intention of telling him. She doubted he'd ever heard of Claxton, New Jersey, but still, he might begin asking questions for conversational purposes and she didn't want to talk about her hometown. "And I'm not talking," she said, glancing away. His eyes were too mesmerizing. They were like a magnet, pulling her in.

At that moment a waitress appeared. "Sorry to keep you waiting. What will you guys have?"

"I want a margarita," she said.

"Please make that two margaritas but hold them until later," Winston added.

Ainsley frowned when the waitress walked off. "Excuse me, but I want my drink now."

"We're about to do something else now."

She tilted her head and tried steadying her heart rate which wasn't easy. "And just what do you think we're about to do?"

"Dance. You said you're not talking so I figured we'll dance first."

Ainsley leaned back in her chair. "And what makes you think I want to dance?"

A smile touched his lips. "I know you want to dance because I noticed you were tapping your feet to the music and even rocking your body a little."

He'd noticed all of that? Jeez, the man was too observant. "I don't need a partner to dance."

"True, but what fun would dancing alone be?"

At that moment the band struck up another number and a rush of people hurriedly moved to the dance floor. "Come on," he said, standing and extending his hand out to her. "Let's dance."

She glanced down at his hand. Should she? She *had* come here to loosen up on the dance floor. Besides, it was a fast number and their bodies wouldn't even touch.

"Unless…"

Ainsley lifted a brow. "Unless what?"

He smiled. "Unless you think you'll embarrass us both out there," he said.

She knew he was only baiting her, but still, she didn't take too kindly to his assertion. If anything, she could probably show him up. In addition to taking dancing classes all her life, she'd also worked part-time as a dancer at a hot spot in New York City, earning extra money while she'd attended journalism school at Columbia University.

She placed her hand in his and the moment their hands touched, she felt her nerve endings ignite. She looked up and met his eyes. It was as if he was staring straight into her soul, seeing things she didn't want anyone to see, especially a stranger. Specifically, she didn't want anyone to know how painful losing the election had been to her.

"Red?"

The man called Winston reclaimed her attention and she fought to ignore the heat sizzling through her veins. The attraction she felt to him was unsettling and she was tempted to pull away her hand but couldn't.

Ainsley stood, tilting her head and meeting his gaze directly. "I'm not afraid of embarrassing you, Winston," she finally responded, saying his name for the first time. "Lead the way."

He lightly tugged on her hand and they moved toward the dance floor. He indicated he wasn't from here and she couldn't help wondering what had brought him to Hilton Head. Was he here trying to escape his troubles like she was, or was he here just to have a good time? She'd glanced at his left hand earlier and noticed he wasn't wearing a ring, nor was there any indication one had recently been on his finger.

When he stopped on the dance floor, she faced him and saw they were standing under the bright lights. The music was lively and funky. The rhythm flowed through her, making her body instinctively move to the beat. She put her all into it.

She noted the surprised look on his face and threw back her head and laughed. Served him right for insinuating she would embarrass him on the dance floor. He laughed as well and then he surprised her when he joined her in the dance, his muscled thighs and broad chest moving in a way that made her insides sizzle. How could such a masculine body move with such grace, style and unfaltering virility? Out of nowhere she remembered hearing that a man who was good on his feet was probably good in bed.

The thought made her nipples harden against her dress and when he eased closer to her and rubbed those muscular thighs against hers, she felt desire flow through her bloodstream, drenching her pores. He continued to surprise her with his dance moves. It seemed they were even. He had pulled one on her, as well.

Ainsley didn't have to be an onlooker to know they danced great together and they looked good as a couple on the dance floor. The room was noisy, the music loud, but none of that mattered. The only thing that attracted her full attention was Winston. She wasn't even sure that was his real name but she would take him at his word. Yet she had no intention of sharing her name with him. If he wanted to continue to call her Red, that was fine with her.

Feeling somewhat feisty she deliberately brushed her body against his. In response, he leaned in close and whispered the words "Naughty Red" in her ear, sending hot waves through her and making a deep longing flare up between her legs. When he moved back to make a turn around the floor, their eyes connected and his penetrating gaze seared her.

She fought for breath when the dance came to an end and he bowed gracefully to her and she smiled. It had been quite a workout. She was about to go back to her table when he captured her hand and asked, "Another?"

Ainsley should have had the mind to decline and return to her seat, especially when the musicians began playing a slow number. Instead she nodded and he gently pulled her into his arms.

She automatically placed her head on his shoulder, not wanting to think about anything but what was happening to her. She had just completed a fast dance with a very handsome, virile and sexy man and now she was on the dance floor in his embrace as their bodies swayed to a slow number.

He tightened his arms around her, bringing her closer to him, and she felt all the contours of his body. She drew in a deep breath and pulled her head away from his shoulder to glance up at him as he moved them in a circular motion around the dance floor. "You didn't tell me you could dance," she whispered accusingly.

Laughing, he showed dimples in both cheeks and she immediately felt her pulse go wacky upon seeing them. "You didn't tell me you could dance, either," he countered.

He was right, she hadn't. There was a lot they were keeping from each other but this was not a night to get serious. It was a night to live life and forget troubles. Besides, there was no reason to get personal. It was just a dance. "I'm not talking, remember?"

He chuckled. "I remember. You don't have to talk but I do want you to feel."

And with those words he drew her deeper into his arms and she could feel the weight of her breasts against his chest and how her nipples tingled with the contact. Then there was the way his hard, muscled thighs brushed against hers while his hand at the center of her back held her close. And she was fully aware every time his lips brushed against her forehead. If he was taking advantage of the soulful, sinfully sultry sound of the music to seduce her, it was working.

Tension curled in the pit of her stomach as the dance became more sensual. A soft gasp escaped from her lips when she felt the hard length of his erection settling indecently between her thighs. She closed her eyes as they moved together in perfect unison, melding their bodies in a lusty configuration around the dance floor. Heat was building between them; she could feel it like a tangible force storming her senses. The man had an intoxicating sensuality that was overwhelming.

They continued to dance and he was effectively wiping all unwanted thoughts from her mind and replacing them with ones too scandalous to think about. She opened her eyes and leaned back to look up at him and his intense gaze captured hers.

She could feel how his body was gliding against hers, igniting pleasure points wherever he brushed her. Her gaze traveled from his eyes to his mouth. She thought it arrogant before but it was sensuous now. His lips had a decadent shape to them, and immediately made her think of kissing... and tasting. She could imagine joining her lips to his while their tongues tangled desperately. Such thoughts made her lips feel dry and she swiped them with the tip of her tongue. She watched his gaze follow the movement.

All too soon she heard the music winding down and reluctantly their bodies parted. He took her hand and led her back to their table. As soon as they were seated, two margaritas were placed in front of them.

"Thanks," she said to the waitress. The woman nodded and smiled before rushing off with the other drinks on her tray.

"Busy night," Winston said smiling.

"Undoubtedly," she said, taking a much-needed sip of her drink.

He was sitting across from her, intently holding her gaze while he sipped his. Sensations began overtaking over and they were sensations she'd never felt before meeting this stranger. There was something about being with this man that prevented her from thinking straight. Prevented her from thinking at all.

She felt dizzy and breathless and drew in a deep breath, trying to control all those lusty thoughts taking over her mind. He reached out and took her hand and smoldering heat suffused her. Why did she feel like a stick of dynamite ready to explode whenever he touched her?

"I'd like to make a suggestion," he said in a deep timbre that continued to wash over her like hot molten desire.

"What kind of suggestion?"

"Come with me."

She swallowed. "And go where?"

"Upstairs. I have a room in this hotel."

Ainsley didn't say anything. She wasn't dumb. She understood his invitation well and knew what would take place in that room. She had come here tonight for a good time, not to tangle between the sheets with a man. But he was making the thought of such a thing incredibly irresistible since he was stroking needs she hadn't taken care of for more than a year now.

She didn't say anything and took another sip of her drink as she continued to watch him with the same intensity that he was watching her. Heat was flowing between them and suddenly she felt an intense need to be alone with him and do what grown folks do.

She didn't have to probe deep into her mind to discover why she was considering his suggestion. She'd been under a lot of strain lately and the election and all the campaigning had wound her up tight. All that negativity had been a crushing blow and she hadn't had a means to escape or regroup. Now it was over and her body was looking for a release.

Maybe a night of mindless, overpowering pleasure was just the thing she needed. Chances were high that she wouldn't see him again since her visit to Hilton Head was short-term.

"Red?"

Lifting her gaze, she tried to fight back sensations that were hurtling around inside her like a violent storm, stroking her needs. She was always someone who hadn't hesitated going after anything she wanted, so why should she hesitate going after him when she did want him?

After taking another sip of her margarita, she set down her glass and said in a breathless quiver, "Okay let's go."

A smile eased to both corners of his lips and his hold on her hand tightened. "All right."

Releasing her hand, he stood to pull out several bills and tossed them on the table to cover their drinks. And when she stood, he placed his hand at her waist as he led her out of the nightclub.

Chapter 3

Winston was grateful he knew his way around the Regency Resort. Holding Red's hand firmly in his, he maneuvered their way past the guest elevators to the private one that would take them directly up to his penthouse suite.

Once or twice when they were forced to slow their pace or else plow into people in front of them, he would take her hand and bring it to his lips. And whenever he glanced over at her, she would give him a heated look that assured him that she was still with him all the way. He definitely appreciated that. Although this was not his first one-night stand and he doubted it would be his last, for some reason getting Red up to his suite was of monumental importance right now.

Red.

Hell, he didn't even know her real name but that didn't matter. The only thing that mattered to him was he wanted her and he wanted her bad. More than he could recall ever wanting a woman before and that was definitely a new experience for him.

Knowing he would be scoring big tonight, he led Red into the elevator. No sooner had the door swooshed closed behind them, he crushed her to him, backed her against the wall and his mouth came charging down. She wrapped her arms around his neck and parted her lips to return his blazing kiss. He actually felt every part of him become on fire.

Liking her taste, he deepened the kiss. His tongue skillfully moved from one side of her mouth to the other, exploring, tasting, stirring sensations he wanted her to feel. Some primitive force was taking over his senses, somehow trying to convince him that she would be different than all his other one-nighters, but for the life of him, he couldn't understand or accept that nonsense. Still, a part of him was helpless to control the raging desire fueling him.

The buzzer went off and he remembered that this was the express elevator, which meant they had gotten to the twentieth floor already. He lifted his head and gazed down at her, taking note of her flushed cheeks, her dilated brown eyes staring at him. He took a step back at the same moment the elevator door opened and quickly stepped out, holding firmly to her hands again.

There were only two suites on this floor and they walked toward the one at the end of the hall. Releasing her hand he pulled the key card from his back pants pocket and then turned to her and said, "I didn't lie. My name is Winston and for the record, I'm not a crazy person or anything. I'm safe."

She nodded. "And for the record, I'm safe as well and you can continue to call me Red."

Obviously she had no intention of giving him a name—first, middle or last. If that's the way she wanted to deal, that was fine with him. The only thing on his mind was making love to her.

"Good enough," he said quickly, inserting his key card in the door. It clicked and he opened it. Taking her hand again, he smiled and said, "Let the good times roll."

He then pulled her inside.

Ainsley recalled getting a fleeting glimpse of Winston's suite before he was all over her, pulling her into his arms and capturing her mouth. The moment their lips locked, his tongue went into action, treating her to all kinds of erotic pleasures while tasting her with openmouthed thoroughness. She'd never been kissed this way before and all coherent thoughts oozed like molten liquid from her brain.

His hands on her backside and thighs had already hiked up her short dress to her waist, and his fingers began working their way underneath the edge of her panties.

Desire was seeping into her pores. It had been a long time since she'd felt a man touch the swelling fullness of her womanhood and the moment he eased a finger between her folds to stroke her clitoris, every part of her began shaking.

This man had a way with his fingers and she clung to him, fearful if she let go he would stop and she didn't want that. His fingers were plunging back and forth inside of her, stroking her in a sensual rhythm, as he licked the corners of her lips with his tongue. Both his fingers and tongue kept an erotic pace until she was certain she would die from the sweet torture.

"Winston…"

She could barely get out his name as his lips trailed along her chin, stopping only for an occasional scrape of his teeth along her jaw.

"Yeah, Red?" he answered in a tone so sexy it made her breath catch.

"I—I want…"

"Tell me what you want. Tonight I'm your delivery man. Whatever you want, I'll deliver. Just tell me."

Evidently the intent was to make her ask…beg or possibly plead, but at that moment, she was past caring. The only thing she wanted was to be taken by him. "I want this," she said, reaching out and tracing her hand against the front of his pants, caressing the hard bulge there. His manhood felt powerful and large and nearly made her weak in the knees. Intense desire had her pressing her legs together at the same time she cupped his groin.

A hand suddenly grasped her jaw. "You sure that's what you want?"

She drew in a deep breath. More desire than she could ever think about was seeping into her pores and triggering an intense throbbing in her womb. "Positive."

From the smile on his face she could only assume he liked her response. In one easy move he took her dress off her body, then he stepped back and she felt the heat of his gaze roam over every inch of her, taking in her red lacy bra and matching panties.

Then he was lifting her in his arms and carrying her across the room to sit her on the high-top table where he quickly proceeded to remove her shoes. In the process he glanced up at her and in a low and guttural tone said, "Just so you'll know, I plan to ride you hard."

Before she could react to what he said, his hand began stroking up her thigh in a way that made her breath shallow. His hands cupped her bare bottom and lifted her to tug down her panties past her hips. The feel of his hands on her backside caused a tingling sensation in her nerve endings.

He leaned close to kiss the waxed flesh covering her femininity, and she felt the tip of his tongue trace a trail along the folds. At that moment she wasn't sure if she would survive his brand of seduction…

But she would die trying.

Winston doubted he'd ever met a more sensuous woman in his entire life. And her scent was doing a number on him, drawing him in and pushing him to take her with an urgency that was driving him insane. And here she sat on his table wearing nothing but a red lacy bra. He couldn't help but take pause to check out the lush curves of her body.

Straightening, he met her gaze seconds before undoing the front clasp of her bra, releasing the most gorgeous twin globes he ever had the pleasure of seeing. He cupped them, used his fingertips to fondle them, causing the nipples to harden before his eyes. He leaned in and with the tip of his tongue, licked them hard before easing them between his lips to suck them hungrily.

Hearing her groan out his name did something to him. He pulled back to look at her and saw passion and desire in the dark depths of her eyes. She was completely naked now and he intended to get naked, as well.

Kicking off his shoes and reaching down to pull off his socks, he straightened and focused his gazed directly on her as he pulled the belt from his slacks and proceeded to ease them down his legs along with his briefs.

He heard her soft gasp when his throbbing manhood was there in full view, and from the look on her face, she appreciated what she saw. Making quick work of removing his shirt, he moved back to her. His hand spanned her small waist, traced a path around her curves and stroked up her back. He leaned closer and asked in a deep, husky voice, "Sure you still want it?" He then took a step back to stare at her.

All Ainsley could do was stare back while every part

of her body throbbed with a need she felt from the top of her head to the soles of her feet. Yes, she still wanted it and refused to think why. From the moment their gazes had connected in the nightclub, something about this man had touched her, sent hot desire rushing all through her blood-stream. She had been sexually drawn to men before, but this one was different. Even now there was something in the depths of his gaze that was making her ache. And he was toting more than a six-pack; the man was so well en-dowed it should be against the law.

"Red?"

He was waiting on her answer? Seriously? Standing in front of her naked, erect as any man could get and he ex-pected any answer other than "bring it on"? Fine. If he wanted an answer then she would give him one. "Yes, just as sure as you're standing there naked with that pointed di-rectly at me," she said of his erection.

He nodded slowly, looking at her beneath gorgeous long lashes. A satisfied smile curved his lips. And before she could draw in her next breath, he swept her off the table into his arms.

Winston headed for the bedroom and once there, he glanced down at her and she looked up at him with those gorgeous brown eyes. And then there was all that hair on her head, those beautiful spiral curls. He liked it. He liked her.

He placed her on the bed and immediately joined her there, going straight for her mouth and kissing her with a hunger that made blood rush all through his body. Shift-ing to move over her, he eased a hard thigh between her soft ones.

Releasing her mouth he went straight for her breasts, re-membering how sweet they'd tasted earlier and devouring them like a starved man. She twisted beneath him and her moans echoed through the room in a heated call of need and desire.

When he lifted her hips, instinctively she wrapped her naked limbs around him and he sucked in a deep breath at the feel of her wet femininity pressed against his flesh. Then in an unexpected move, she slipped from beneath him and pushed him onto his back.

Their gazes locked for a brief moment before she lowered her head between his legs and took him into her mouth.

"Oh hell…"

Those were the only words he could groan from his lips before a tirade of sensations swept over him. He reached out and grabbed hold of the mass of her hair but she kept her mouth fixed on him. No matter how much he tugged, she wouldn't let him go.

The woman was letting him have it, feasting on him, and making him groan out words he probably wouldn't remember in the morning. He felt as if every inch of his skin was electrified, unbelievably sensitized. A multitude of new sensations, some he'd never experienced before, flooded his body as she licked her tongue over every inch of him.

And when he felt his body about to explode he tried pushing her away, but she locked her mouth down on him with the steely pressure of a suction cup, refusing to let him hold anything back.

"Red!"

His body quaked, shivering in a release so profound and powerful he felt pushed way over the edge. A different kind of intensity fired his loins and a sense of awareness labored down hard on him. Not being able to take her brand of torture any longer, he reached under his pillow to retrieve the condom package he'd put there earlier when he'd assumed Sophie would be his bedmate.

He quickly slipped on the condom with the experience

of a man who'd done this, with or without a female audience, a number of times.

She automatically lifted her hips when he moved to settle between them. The scent of their aroused bodies filled the air like an aphrodisiac, intoxicating him, destroying the last shred of self-control he might have had.

Effectively pushed over the edge with no return, he slid fully inside her, going deep and filling her with every aroused inch of him. She let out a deep moan and her legs tightened around him, pulling him in deeper.

Winston began moving, establishing a rhythm, and the sound of flesh against flesh mingled with their moans, filling the room. He'd warned her that he would take her hard and he wasn't backing down. Every thrust into her body was with a purpose, meant to drive them closer to the satisfaction they both urgently sought.

She screamed the exact moment his body bucked as intense spasms tore through him. He murmured something, not sure exactly what, as he tilted her hips at an angle that would make her aware of just how deep inside her he was.

Screaming again, her inner muscles clamped down and triggered a multitude of sensations that had his body convulsing. This was one hell of a sexual mating and he doubted he would ever forget it.

She dragged in a deep, quivering breath and he adjusted his position to lie beside her and draw her into his arms. "I got this room for two days. Stay with me."

She leaned back and looked up at him. "Stay here?"

"Yes. You're on the island alone, right?" he asked her.

"Yes."

"So am I, so there's no reason we can't spend another day and night together."

Ainsley was about to tell him that she could think of several reasons. But that was before he leaned down and claimed a nipple with his mouth, shooting all kinds of sensations through her. "Say you'll stay," he murmured against her lips.

She was about to tell him there was no way she could stay, but then he lowered his hands to the juncture of her thighs. His fingers began caressing her womanly core, igniting new sensations to stir within her and causing sexual need lined with anticipation to strip her senses. At that moment she couldn't turn him down for anything. Somehow in between gasps of pleasure she murmured, "I'll stay."

Chapter 4

The next morning Ainsley opened her eyes when she heard the sound of the shower. It was time to make her break. She'd only pretended to be sleeping and now she needed to get the hell out of there.

Scooting off the bed, she looked around for her bra, found it and swiftly put it on. Leaving the bedroom, she found her dress and panties where they had been taken off her. Wiggling into her dress she wadded up her panties and quickly shoved them into her purse while sliding her feet into her shoes. Time was of the essence and she was determined to be gone before Winston got out of the shower.

Winston.

For crying out loud, she had spent the entire night with a man and she didn't even know his full name. But then, she thought, hurriedly moving toward the door, he knew none of hers, so what did that say about him?

At some point last night she recalled him asking her to

spend the day and another night with him and she'd fool-
ishly agreed. But now that she had reclaimed all her senses,
there was no way she would spend two nights of marathon
sex with a man she didn't know. It was bad enough she had
spent one night with him.

Before opening the door, she glanced around, really seeing the suite for the first time. It was humongous, nearly
twice the size of her condo back in New York. She wondered
what he did for a living to afford such extravagances. Last
night she'd been too busy to appreciate the elegance of the
oceanfront two-bedroom suite with its separate living and
dining rooms, as well as a nice kitchen nook with a high-
top table and chairs.

Ainsley blushed when she remembered what they'd done
on that table, which was why she needed to leave now.
Winston whatever-his-name had the ability to make her do
things she normally didn't do…like one-night stands. And
then to agree to spend a day and another night with him,
undoubtedly for more of the same mind-blowing sex. There
was no doubt in her mind it would be enjoyable, but then
her brain cleared from all that pleasure and she recalled that
he had had condoms stashed under his pillow. That meant
he had intended to bring some woman back here last night
for a treat and she'd been the willing delicacy.

Easing shut the door behind her, she swiftly walked toward the elevator, ignoring the curious looks from an older
couple who were stepping out of it. She didn't need a mirror
to realize all those passion marks on the side of her face,
neck and upper chest were visible to the naked eye. She
hoped she could make it out of the hotel and to the parking
lot without too many people staring. It was early morning
and she was wearing the outfit from last night as if she was
ready to go partying. If the Claxton news reporter Luis had
paid to dog her heels all during the election were to see her

now, he would certainly have a story. She could just imagine the headlines: *Ainsley St. James spent the night with a man she didn't know.*

You couldn't get any more scandalous than that, she thought, finally leaving the hotel without making a spectacle of herself. A few moments later she was in her car and driving away, and it was only then that she released the breath she'd been holding.

It wouldn't be so bad if every cell in her body didn't vibrate from all the memories that were flowing through her head, memories her mind just refused to let go of. Like how with Winston's help she had managed to quench a feverish hunger that had been inside her, a hunger she hadn't known she'd had until he had exposed it in the most delectable way. Even now her nipples were jutting hard against her dress in memory of how much attention he'd given them.

Not to be outdone, the area between her legs was twitching, remembering how his hands, mouth and shaft had invaded her in a way that she would never forget. It had taken coming to Hilton Head to meet a man capable of making her scream at the top of her lungs.

Glancing at the clock on her car's console, she was surprised to see it wasn't quite seven in the morning, as she continued driving toward the Inner Harbor Resort. She tried not to think about what Winston's reaction would be when he walked out of the shower and found her gone.

As it stood now, he didn't know a single thing about her and that was a good thing since last night meant nothing to either of them. There was no doubt in her mind that women came and went from his bed in a steady stream.

As for her, she would spend the next ten days relaxing, and then at some point she needed to call her former employer to try and get her old job back as a journalist for *The New York Times.*

She had resigned from her job in August of last year, certain she would win the election because she had the backing of the entire town. Besides, at the time it had been an uncontested race. So to her way of thinking, it should have been a sure win for her. However, at the last minute, Higgins, a newcomer to town, had made a surprise move and thrown his hat into the ring. In no time at all his campaign had strategized by going after her character, literally cutting it into threads.

The election in November had been a shocker since Higgins had won by a landslide victory. She had been ready to pack up and leave Claxton and return to New York, and would have done so had it not been for her father's heart attack the day after the election.

Ainsley was certain the negative campaign had taken a toll on her parents, her father in particular since she was a *daddy's girl*. She felt somehow responsible and since she was her parents' only child, she'd remained in Claxton for the past two months during her father's recuperation period. Now he was a lot better and had returned to work last week.

And it was time for her to do the same.

As she continued to drive to the resort, her mind drifted and she couldn't help remembering last night. Why hadn't she listened to her best friend, Tessa Spencer? Tessa had warned her the Sparrow would be full of men with only one thing on their mind. Your cookie. "Unless you're prepared for them to gobble it up, then go someplace else," Tessa had said. But Ainsley had gone anyway. It wasn't that she hadn't believed Tessa. She hadn't placed a lot of significance on the warning because she'd been certain she could handle any situation. She was a big girl and could take care of herself.

Only thing for certain, she hadn't been prepared for the likes of Winston what's-his-name and last night he had been hers completely. Every single sexy, make-a-woman-drool part of him. And she had acted like a greedy hussy. It didn't take much to remember how those dark eyes would stare her down with that I-want-to-make-love-to-you look, stimulating within her a need she hadn't known existed.

Her hand tightened on the steering wheel when she brought the rental car to a stop at a traffic light. Then there were those naughty messages he'd whispered in her ear right after they'd made love that first time when he held her in his arms. They had made her breathless anticipating him doing just what he said he would do. And he had. With an experience she didn't want to wonder how he got, he had used his tongue to taste every part of her body, inch by sensual inch. He seemed especially partial to her breasts. But then other parts of her hadn't been neglected, either.

While he'd been atop her, stroking into her body in a rhythm that nearly drove her insane, she had looked up at him and seen the intense expression in the hard angles and planes of his face. She had gotten absorbed in the deep, dark eyes staring back at her as he sent her over the edge. His lovemaking had been so profound it took her breath away just thinking about it. He had definitely been her fantasy.

Now it was back to reality. As she turned into the entry gates to the resort, she decided that she would shower and go to bed and get the sleep she'd been deprived of last night.

Leaving the bathroom after his shower, Winston didn't have to look at the empty bed to know Red was gone. She had agreed to stay for another day and night and he had been looking forward to it. He figured he should be grateful she had left, but couldn't help feeling disappointed that she had left without first telling him…

What? Her name? How to contact her again?

He rubbed his hand down his face in frustration. He didn't handle one-nighters that way. Usually he would have a name, a first one at least, although most of the time he wasn't certain it was genuine. And he'd never felt the need to keep one woman around. So why had he tried making Red different?

Because she was.

The moment he had eased between her legs and thrust hard inside of her, he'd known it. Never had he engaged in such mindless, erotic pleasure. Her inner muscles had clenched him, nearly made him beg for mercy, and driven him to make his strokes harder. Pound into her deeper. She would scream and he would growl.

And then her going down on him was no joke, either. What she'd done with her mouth had shudders running up his spine even now. He had known when he'd seen her at the club that her mouth could deliver and it had. She'd given him mindless pleasure and had ignited something wild and untamed inside him, making him want to go another round, then another, and another.

Hell, it had definitely been one incredible night.

Now she was gone and chances were he would never see her again.

He moved toward the bed and glanced around. There wasn't a trace of her anywhere. But all he had to do was sniff the air to inhale her lingering scent. It was an aroma that hadn't just entrenched in the air but was embedded in his skin even after his shower. The woman had worked her way into his mind.

A fierce frown settled on his face and he drew in a deep breath while giving his mind a mental dressing-down. *Then you need to get her out of your mind. She was a one-nighter, so why are you getting so worked up about it? You don't do relationships, don't have time and wouldn't do one if you did. Do you need to be reminded of Caroline Darling and all the pain she caused you?*

Yes, at that moment he needed to be reminded of Caroline, and the memory was like a douse of ice water to his body. It didn't matter that his night with Red had been off the charts. Great sex was great sex but that was all it was. No woman would get under his skin again no matter how great the sex was.

A short while later Winston was glad he'd managed to get his mind back in check. He had dressed to go down for breakfast and play a game of golf when his cell phone went off. He could tell by the ring it was Uriel. Each of his godbrothers had their own ring tone. Uriel happened to be the oldest of the six, besting Winston's thirty-four by eighteen months.

Most people knew the story as to how six guys had become best friends while attending Morehouse and had on graduation day made a pact to stay in touch by becoming godfathers to each other's children, and that the first-born sons' names would carry the letters of the alphabet from U to Z. And that was how Uriel Lassiter, Virgil Bougard, Winston Coltrane, Xavier Kane, York Ellis and Zion Blackstone had come into existence.

Winston was close to his godparents and godbrothers and couldn't imagine them not being a part of his life…although at the moment he was somewhat annoyed with three of them: Uriel, Xavier and York.

A few years ago when he and all five of his godbrothers were going through some sort of issues with women, they had come up with the idea of the Bachelors in Demand Club. They were supposed to be die-hard players—all six of them—who would enjoy life without any serious entanglements. But now the club of six was down to three after Uriel, Xavier and York had fallen in love and married. As far as he was concerned they were all whipped men.

It didn't matter one iota that he happened to like the

women his three godbrothers had married. That was beside the point. The fact remained that they had defected.

"What's up, U?" Over the years they had shortened their names for each other to just the first letter.

"I haven't heard from you since the New Year's Eve party. Just checking on you, W."

He wasn't surprised since he and his godbrothers stayed in contact pretty regularly. "I'm fine. How's Ellie doing?" Uriel's wife was expecting their first child in May. Xavier's wife, Farrah, was expecting that month, as well. Winston had to get used to the idea of U and X as fathers, just like he'd gotten used to them as married men.

"Ellie's fine. She's working on another novel and believes this one will be a bestseller."

"They always are." Ellie was a romance author who wrote under the pseudonym of Flame Elbam. Uriel and Ellie hosted a New Year's Eve party every year at their home in Cavanaugh Lake in North Carolina. It had been at that party a couple of weeks ago that Ellie had announced her last novel had been on *The New Yorks Times* Bestseller List for six weeks straight.

"I hear you're off Barrett Shores for a few days," Uriel said.

Winston didn't have to guess where U had gotten that information. More than likely it had come from York since he had been the last one Winston had spoken with. York had called this morning when Winston was throwing items into an overnight bag.

It hadn't been loneliness that had driven Winston across the Sound to Hilton Head. The need to get laid had been the driving factor. And the trip hadn't been disappointing.

"Yes, I needed to come into town," he heard himself saying.

"How are things going with the project?"

Up until a month ago, very few people had known that his research as a marine biologist had reached a major breakthrough in the medical arena. Since word had somehow gotten leaked to the press, he'd been inundated with emails and letters wanting interviews.

"Pain in the ass right now. I prefer keeping my hands in the research side of things versus the business side, you know that."

"Yes, and you should have taken my advice and hired a public relations expert. It's only a matter of time before your true identity gets out and Barrett Shores won't be your private island anymore."

Winston frowned at the thought. When he had left his six-figure job with Destin Pharmaceuticals a few years back, he had decided to further his research under a pseudonym to keep his private life private. And following Ellie's advice, he'd even gone so far as to set up a Facebook page with a picture of his grandfather for publicity purposes to appease the serious diggers determined to uncover his true identity. However, Uriel was right. Pretty soon some determined reporter would dig deep enough and find out Winston Coltrane and the renowned Dr. R. J. Chambers were one and the same.

He and Uriel talked for a few minutes more, ending with their plan for all the godbrothers to join York and his wife Darcy in New York next month over Valentine's Day weekend when the couple would celebrate their first wedding anniversary.

As he walked down the corridor to the elevator, he could still smell Red's scent and knew it would remain with him for a long time whether he wanted it to or not.

Chapter 5

"So, how are things going?"

Ainsley smiled upon hearing Tessa's voice. "Fine. I'm stretched out on the beach watching the waves come in. It's so relaxing. I wish you could have come with me," she said, pulling up in a sitting position.

"I wish I could have come, too, but some of us have to work for a living."

Ainsley groaned, thinking of her own employment situation. "And some of us are unemployed."

"Have you called *The New York Times* to see if you can get your old job back?" Tessa asked her.

"I put in a call to Bobby a few days ago and he hasn't returned it. The last time we talked, I was lectured on how the company was reducing their staff so he couldn't make me any promises. I knew when I resigned that the downsizing was due to the economy. However, at the time, I was so sure I was going to win the election and wouldn't need that job."

"And you would have, if Luis Higgins hadn't lied about you being a stripper instead of a dancer at that New York club during your college days."

"Doesn't matter." She wouldn't admit it to Tessa but it had mattered. The good people of Claxton, many of whom she'd known all her life, had let her down by believing such nonsense. They had been quick to believe the worst and decided a mayor with a history of pole dancing just wouldn't cut it, regardless of the fact it was one of her ancestors, the first Ainsley St. James, who had founded the town and had been the town's first mayor.

"I'm hoping Bobby calls me back before I leave. I want to have some definite plans in place before returning to Claxton. With Luis Higgins as mayor, I won't stay in town any longer than I have to. Dad is doing better so he doesn't need me any more. I'll return just long enough to pack my bags. Mom and Dad understand."

Ainsley was glad she had sub-leased her New York condo in Harlem. The couple had only wanted a six-month lease, which meant she had a place to stay when she returned. However, with this trip and the personal money she'd thrown into the campaign, she needed an income to pay her bills.

"So, have you run into *Mr. Hot-Throb* any more?"

She'd told Tessa about meeting Winston at the nightclub a week ago, but she hadn't told her anything about spending the night with him. That was too much to share with anyone, even a best friend. "No, I haven't run into him. He's probably left the island already."

She couldn't help wondering if he had. She hadn't gone back to the Sparrow, but she had gone to a couple restaurants on that side of town. And she'd always felt the need to look over her shoulder, nervous about running into him again.

It was hard to believe it had been a week already. She

hated admitting there hadn't been one single day that she hadn't thought about Winston—remembering something he had said or recalling how he would look at her with those dark penetrating eyes of his.

Some days a part of her wished she hadn't sneaked out of his hotel room like a thief in the night. It would have been nice to have spent the morning after with him, possibly even sharing breakfast if nothing more. Then on other days she was convinced she had done the right thing. One-night stands didn't need to extend into the next day and night. It was best to make a clean break and move on.

She had ended her phone call with Tessa, gone back to her room to shower and change for dinner at one of the resort's restaurants when her cell phone rang again. Her heart kicked up a beat when she saw it was her old boss, Bobby Ryerson. "Bobby, I was wondering if you were going to call me back."

"Hey, kid, I didn't want to interrupt your vacation until I could deliver good news."

"And you can?" she asked, crossing her fingers. She needed her old job back. The sooner she could return to New York and the life she'd had there the better.

"Sort of. Like I told you, with the economy the way it is the paper isn't hiring or doing rehires…except for special projects. I think I've come up with a freelance piece I can bring you back to write if you're interested."

"What's it about?"

"Not what but who. Ever heard of Dr. R. J. Chambers?"

A frown burrowed her brow. "No."

"But you have heard of the prescription drug Norjamin."

"Yes, although it's still pending approval by the FDA, it's the drug that's supposed to run rings around Viagra. I've heard it's better all the way around with minimum side effects."

"That's good news *all the way around*, and Chambers is the marine biologist who was the mastermind behind that pill. His identity is a heavily guarded secret. The only thing anyone knows about him is from what's going through social media. But I have a lead that Chambers is working on this remote island off Hilton Head. I want to put you on it right away. The paper will cover everything."

"Okay." Additional time on Hilton Head wouldn't be so bad, especially when the last weather report indicated it was snowing in New York. "For how long?"

"At least three weeks. We want you to get inside his head. Get the scoop on his next project. Find out why he prefers living the life of a recluse. And it'd be ideal if we could put something in print around Valentine's Day weekend, when sex is on a lot of people's minds."

Ainsley rolled her eyes. "I believe it's romance that's on everyone's mind on that day."

"Same thing."

Deciding not to give her opinion on that, especially after her recent one-night stand, she said. "I need an address."

"Does that mean you're going to do it?" Bobby asked and she could hear the smile in his voice.

"Like you didn't think I would. But I have a few stipulations," she said, pulling the hotel notepad out of the drawer.

"You know I can't promise you anything, St. James."

She didn't believe that for one minute. "I want my old job back, Bobby—including my office and weekly column."

"You resigned, so sure that you were going to win that election, and we hired someone else."

He was right. She had thought she would win. Deciding to use another approach, she said. "My replacement is doing a piss-poor job with that column and you and I both know it. I read the reviews."

Bobby let out a deep sigh. "Giving you your old job back won't be that easy. She's the niece of someone at the top."

Ainsley nervously gnawed on her bottom lip. In that case, it wouldn't be easy but not impossible. "I'll give you what you want from Chambers and you work on getting me what I want."

Bobby didn't say anything for a minute and then, "You deliver the goods on Chambers and I'll see what I can do. And I need a newsbreaker, St. James. Chambers has been a recluse on that island. So far we're the only ones who've gotten a lead as to where he lives so we need to move fast. It's going to be up to you to convince the old man to do the interview."

"Wait! Hold up! Are you saying Chambers hasn't agreed to talk to me?"

"Not just you, he hasn't agreed to talk to anyone. I understand he prefers the solitude with all those sea creatures. He doesn't have a life. In fact, he doesn't even know anyone has discovered his whereabouts. Chances are he won't be too happy when you show up, but hopefully you can soften up the old man."

She frowned. "I appreciate the vote of confidence."

"No problem and if you get discouraged, just remember that this story makes you one step closer to reclaiming your old job, including your office and your column." He quickly added, "But I can't make promises."

Ainsley smiled. "Too late, Bobby. You just did. Get the presses ready. I plan on giving you one hell of a scoop."

Chapter 6

Ainsley brought her car to a stop and glanced at the huge sign. *Entering Barrett Shores. You're not welcome unless you were invited.*

Well, she thought. You couldn't get any clearer than that. She then looked ahead at the bridge in front of her, the one that would take her across the Port Royal Sound to the island. The first question that came to her mind was whether or not it was safe. It was made of wood and the planks didn't look sturdy enough to hold a cart much less a car. But tire tracks ingrained in the wooden surface over time indicated vehicles had driven across without making the old bridge come tumbling down. She compressed her lips deciding she would take her chances. What choice did she have if she wanted her old job back?

Humming "Nearer, My God, to Thee," she put her car in Drive and slowly moved ahead. As soon as her front tire touched the plank, she held her breath and tried taking her mind off the lack of sturdiness of the bridge by noticing the beauty of the surrounding area. Through the tall oak trees peeked the blue-green of the Atlantic Ocean. The view was simply breathtaking.

She released a sigh of relief when she made it off the bridge and lifted her head to give thanks. Hopefully, she'd be going back across before dark. If old man Chambers didn't agree to the interview she would be leaving the island a lot sooner than that. Refusing to consider he wouldn't do the interview, she squared her shoulders and drove on, following the one-lane road that, according to her GPS, would lead her right to the sanctuary where Dr. R. J. Chambers lived and worked. She had spent the last two days trying to get as much information on the man as she could. There had been plenty, on his Facebook page and in Wikipedia. Both of those had provided a picture of a distinguished-looking man in his late sixties or early seventies. However, nothing she'd researched had provided anything else about his identity and whereabouts. Bobby was right. The man was living the life of a recluse.

She rounded a curve in the road and quickly brought the car to a stop when her breath caught. "Wow!"

Ainsley wasn't exactly sure what she had expected of Chambers's home but it definitely hadn't been this. The view while driving across the bridge had been spectacular, but this here was so magnificent it actually left her breathless.

Tucked away amid the tallest oak trees she'd ever seen was a sprawling three-story house with over eight hundred feet of beachfront. It was early January, yet all the leaves were a deep evergreen. It was as if spring had come early here while some places farther north were snow covered.

The house itself looked as if it could hold four or five families easily. But she figured most of the rooms were where Dr. Chambers did his work. The man usually published a book every eighteen months, in addition to being a regular contributor to numerous marine publications. But the drug before the FDA was rumored to be his biggest achievement yet and already several pharmaceutical companies wanted his named linked to their corporation. So far he had committed to none.

Her gaze traveled to the sky, saw the strength of the sun and how it appeared to kiss the blue-green waters of the ocean. She could imagine waking up to such a view every morning. The old man was a recluse and now she could see why. If she had this at her fingertips, she would never leave the island, either. She could imagine sitting on the docks nursing a margarita while enjoying the view of endless water. She wasn't surprised that a man, successful in the study of eliminating sexual dysfunction, would live on a private island like a king.

After parking the car, she got out and glanced around. She expected a member of Chambers's staff to appear and tell her that she was trespassing. When it became obvious no one would be there to intercept her, she began walking around the gate trying to find a good place to enter. After risking her life by driving across that bridge, there was no way she was leaving without attempting to see Dr. Chambers.

Winston muttered a curse when the buzzer went off in his lab. Someone was on his property. He pushed away from the huge aquarium and angrily snatched the work gloves off his hands. He was in the middle of cleaning out one of his tanks and there was no reason to get interrupted. Evidently someone hadn't read the huge sign before crossing the bridge. It wasn't the first time and it wouldn't be the last. He had thought about removing the bridge completely, which meant he could only use his boat whenever he needed to get to Hilton Head or Parris Island. But why should he be inconvenienced because someone refused to adhere to his wishes?

Ignoring the dolphins flipping around in the huge tank as he passed by, he checked his watch. It would be feeding time for them soon and, with all he had to do, he should stay on schedule. He moved into the lobby of his work area and picked up the remote to turn on the nearest security monitor. A flat screen mounted on the wall flared to life and he immediately saw the car parked on the west side of his property.

Switching to other security channels, he didn't see a thing. York, a former officer for the NYPD, who owned a high-tech security firm in New York, had installed the state-of-the-art system himself. And knowing how much of a stickler York was to detail, it would be just a matter of time before Charley discovered the location of his intruder.

Charley was the name he'd given the talking security system that had the capability of scanning not only every inch of the island but up to one hundred feet of the waterways, to alert him of any intruders arriving by boat, as well. At first it had been hard getting used to the talking device since it seemed to have a mind of its own at times. It reminded him of Kitt, the voice of the talking Trans Am in the *Knight Rider* TV series.

"Warning. Warning," Charley blasted. *"Trespasser. East grounds."*

"Scan perimeters, Charley," Winston ordered, switching out of his work shoes into a pair of Nike shoes.

"Vehicle located. Rental. Currently empty."

"Tell me something I haven't figured out for myself," he muttered to the machine.

Charley's light began flashing. *"Repeat command. Didn't understand. Failed communication."*

Winston rolled his eyes. "Find trespasser and scan."

He was halfway through the door when Charley blasted out the information. *"Found. Female. East grounds."*

Winston nodded as he went toward the door. So his intruder was a woman. Well, she had a lot of explaining to do. Not only had she crossed the bridge to his property when she should not have, but somehow she had gotten through the east gate. The only way she could have done that was by picking the lock.

"Notify authorities?" Charley asked.

"No" was Winston's single response before stepping out the door. Whoever the brazen woman was, he would handle her himself.

Making his way to the balcony, he saw a glimpse of her as she quickly crossed the east patio. He took the stairs two at a time as he moved up to the main floor. Easing open the French doors, he stood concealed by several huge plants. It would only be a matter of time before she came dashing his way.

Suddenly, there was a stirring in the pit of his groin and he wondered why. Then he knew. His nostrils had picked up a scent and it was the same fragrance that had remained with him for the past week and a half. The same scent he woke to each morning and went to bed with at night. The scent of the woman whose memory just wouldn't leave him.

Red.

A fine time for his imagination to run wild, he thought. Steeling his mind against the scent he wished like hell he could forget, he pressed against the wall, determined that whoever she was, she wouldn't slip past him. Out of the corner of his eye, he saw a slender figure and then a flash of blue. And then as if on cue, he emerged from his hiding place and grabbed her by the arm, bringing her body to his. "Look, lady, this is private property. You have no right to be here. And you're leaving now!"

She fought, trying to reclaim her arm but he held tight in an attempt to drag her back to where her car was parked.

"Let go of me, you ass."

Something about that voice, as well as the scent that continued to corrode his senses, made him loosen his hold on her at the same time she swung around and lifted her foot to deliver a firm kick in his groin. He jumped out of the way and his jaw dropped when he saw her face. "Red?"

She gasped and froze when she pushed all that hair from her face. Shock etched her features and rendered her speechless for a moment. Finally she regained her voice. "Winston?"

He continued to stare at her while struggling to decipher just why she was there. Seeing her again did something to him. It was as if a keg of dynamite filled with lust suddenly exploded inside his entire body. Without thinking, he reached out, pulled her close and captured her mouth with his.

Ainsley had intended to shove him away, bite his tongue, or scream in protest…however, she did none of those things. The moment her senses reacquainted with his taste, a taste she hadn't been able to forget, there was nothing she could do but stand there and moan.

And while doing so she disregarded everything, including the way his hands moved all over her body, over her curves, cupping her backside and tightening around her waist. Instead his touch compelled her to react—so she did, by kissing him back and wrapping her arms around his neck.

This was insane. This was madness. Totally crazy. She

knew this and figured he knew it as well, but something was driving them to lose themselves in this kiss.

The intensity of it increased and she felt his hand ease up the back of her blouse to touch her skin. The moment he did, her flesh felt scorched from the heat of his fingers.

Suddenly he broke off the kiss and gazed down at her, his eyes filled with as much desire as they had on their night together. He reached out a hand and used his fingertips to trace a trail across her moist lips. "I hadn't expected you to come looking for me, but I'm glad you did. And since you're here, let's not waste any time."

What? Did he actually think she had come here looking for him? He moved closer and drew her to him again, intending to get another kiss. She shoved him away. "I didn't come here for this…or for you."

She could actually see the look of surprise in the dark depths of his eyes. "You didn't?"

"Of course not."

He lifted a brow. "Of course not?"

"Yes," she said straightening her blouse and tucking it back inside her jeans and then smoothing her hair. "Why would you think such a thing?"

Why indeed? Winston thought, leaning back against the brick wall and regarding her intently. He liked the way she did that, fluff all that hair from her face with a single flick of her wrist. He thought she looked good in jeans, just as good as she had in a dress. Almost. He liked seeing her legs. But then, it seemed that no matter what she put on those luscious curves of hers, it could set his body on fire.

"Well?"

He glanced away from those curves and up to her face. "Well, what?"

She placed her hands on her hips and shifted her legs in one of those I'm-ready-to-take-you-on stances. "What made you think I came here looking for you? In fact, that night, you led me to believe you weren't from Hilton Head."

Winston placed his arms across his chest. "I'm not. This is Barrett Shores, an island separate from Hilton Head. And it's private property and you're here uninvited. Sex was good between us that night, so what else am I to think other than you came looking for me?"

Ainsley frowned. The man had an oversize ego. She had no intentions of stroking it by agreeing to how good the sex was. "I'm not here to see you. I'm here to see Dr. Chambers."

He dropped his hands to his side, straightened from the wall and lifted a brow. "Dr. Chambers?"

"Yes."

After pausing a moment, he asked, "And what is your business with him?"

She narrowed her eyes. "What are you, his bodyguard?"

Winston inwardly smiled. She didn't know just how close to the truth that was. "Yes, I'm his bodyguard and you need to state your business with me."

She rolled her eyes. "Fine." She then opened the small pouch around her neck and pulled out a business card. "Here. Now if you'll just let him know I'd like to meet with him, I would appreciate it."

Winston studied the card she handed him. *Ainsley St. James, News Reporter, The New York Times*. He glanced back at her. Ainsley? Her real name was Ainsley? He smiled, liking it already.

"What's so funny?" she asked in a waspish tone.

He wiped the smile off this face. "Nothing."

He then glanced back down at the card…at her occupation again. She was a reporter? Aw, hell. Winston immediately thought about his brother Evan who'd played in the NFL. A couple years back Evan had fallen for some reporter who had only wanted a story. She had pretended affection for Evan while doing an exposé on NFL players' use of steroids. Although Evan's reputation hadn't gotten damaged by the story, several of his teammates' had and he'd felt partly to blame. Winston recalled his brother's pain at the woman's betrayal and he had made up in his mind after that episode to never get involved with a reporter.

He glanced back at her and slid the business card in the pocket of his shirt. "Come on, I'll walk you back to your car," he said, taking hold of her arm.

She dug in her heels. "Wait! I can't leave yet. I told you I'm here to see Dr. Chambers."

"He doesn't want to see you."

She crossed her arms over her chest and glared at him. "How would you know?"

"I know because he doesn't do reporters."

"I understand that. I also know he's gone to great lengths to keep his whereabouts hidden and all."

"Yes, he has," Winston replied, and then one dark brow rose. "And that has me wondering how you found him."

She blew out a deep breath. "Surely you don't expect me to expose my sources."

"Yes, I do. Either to me or Chambers. Either way he won't see you."

"Then I want to hear it from him."

"He's busy."

"I'll wait. You're his bodyguard, not his spokesman."

Winston chuckled as he leaned back against the wall again. "He values anything I tell him, trust me." Every muscle in his body went rigid when a suspicion Winston didn't like floated across his mind. Had she been on to him that night? He looked at her and frowned. "That night you told me you were in Hilton Head on a vacation."

"I was for two weeks. My boss called and since I was in the area, he offered me a chance to do the interview."

And it was an interview she wouldn't be getting. "I really don't know what to tell you, Red, but Chambers—"

"My name is Ainsley. You know it now so use it," she said harshly.

He smiled. The woman was feisty but then he'd known that. That night they'd practically had a sex marathon and she had bit him a couple times with her teeth, clawed his back with her nails and nearly sucked him dry with her mouth. Winston felt a tightening in his gut when he remembered the latter. She had gone down on him in a way no other woman had. His gaze lowered to her mouth. He loved that mouth. It was sexy with full lips. He loved kissing it, tonguing it, nibbling on it…and he also enjoyed what she could do with it.

"Winston?"

He glanced back at her eyes. "Yes, *Ainsley*?"

Ainsley drew in a sharp breath. *Why did he have to say her name like that? Like it was a breathless whisper from his lips combined with a husky groan from deep within his throat.* And then there were those penetrating dark eyes that could take your breath away, hypnotize you into thinking about doing all sorts of naughty things.

"I need you to put in a good word for me with Dr. Chambers." She didn't want to beg and she wouldn't. She would just ask nicely. If he had any pull with Chambers then she needed whatever leverage she could get.

She watched the way his mouth twitched in a slow grin showing those same dimples that had turned her on that night. Those same dimples that were turning her on now.

Ainsley turned away to glance out at the ocean. It was beautiful from here. She bet the view was simply gorgeous from anywhere on this island. She glanced back at Winston and thought, yes, he was a bodyguard and he would make a good one. He was definitely physically fit with muscles galore. She could recall running her hands over his biceps plenty of times that night. She doubted there was an area of his body she hadn't touched…or tasted.

She glanced away again, not ready to recall just what they had shared and how deeply they'd shared it. She hadn't acted herself that night. She had let loose, which was something she didn't do often. She had needed it. And it had definitely helped. Other than when visions of him would creep into her dreams, she'd been sleeping like a baby since.

She forced her gaze back to him. He hadn't responded one way or the other. Hadn't he heard her? "Winston, I asked if you—"

"I heard you."

She shrugged. "I wasn't sure since you didn't say anything."

"I was thinking."

"Oh."

He was still staring at her and she wondered what thoughts were going through his mind. Hopefully, they weren't the same ones that had been going through hers. Sometimes it was best to move forward and not look back. In their case, she knew it to be true.

"I'll call you tomorrow with my answer," he said, breaking into both her thoughts and the silence.

She frowned. "Tomorrow? But I wanted to talk to him today."

"That won't be happening. If he agrees to see you then I'll call you."

"And if he doesn't?"

"Then I won't. It's just an interview. If you can't interview him, then I'm sure you can move on to someone else.

I hear George Clooney will be on the island sometime this week."

She shook her head. "You don't understand. I need to do a story on Dr. Chambers. I've been assigned to get an interview from him."

Winston drew in a deep breath. "It's going to be hard for him to agree. Like I told you, he doesn't do interviews."

"Then I need for you to make sure I'm his first."

He tilted his head and looked at her. "And why should I do that, Ainsley?"

She shrugged and then said, "Because we're friends?"

He held her gaze steadily. "No, we're not friends. As you reminded me earlier, it was just sex that night. Friends don't have sex. Come on, I'll walk you to your car."

Deciding not to push, she walked with him to where her car was parked, not saying anything. They walked slowly and she was fighting hard to force back the desire that was pounding deep inside her. What was there about him that could make her want to do crazy stuff? She glanced down at his outfit, a brown shirt and a pair of khaki walking shorts. He had nice legs.

She cleared her throat deciding to strike up a conversation, since her car was parked on the other side of the estate. "Nice place."

Instead of answering, he nodded. She decided to ask something that would elicit a response. "Have you worked for Dr. Chambers long?"

He glanced over at her. "Long enough."

At least that was a start. "How long?"

"Several years."

Ainsley didn't say anything for a minute and then asked, "Is there only the two of you here?"

He lifted a brow. "Why do you want to know?"

"Curious."

"Curious or nosy?" he asked as they went down some steps. He touched her elbow to assist her and desire flared to life within her again.

"A little of both, I guess. After all, I am a reporter."

He didn't say anything for a minute and then announced, "Charley's here, too."

"Charley?"

"Yes."

"What does he do?"

"Security. He runs the command center. Any time someone shows up on this property uninvited, Charley lets us know."

This time she nodded. "I'm looking forward to meeting both Charley and Dr. Chambers." He didn't say anything as he opened the car door for her but she made no move to get inside just yet. He had an unreadable expression on his face and Ainsley didn't know if she could depend on him being an ally or not.

"If you really want to meet Chambers, then maybe you need to think about what I'll want out of this," he said, breaking into her thoughts.

His words spurred a tightness in the pit of her stomach. "What do you mean?"

"I think you know what I mean."

She had a sinking feeling that she did, but in situations like this it behooved a person to play dumb. "I don't really so please clarify."

"No problem." He moved in close, brought his face down to hers. "You want something from me and I want something from you."

He was so close that it wouldn't take much for him to kiss her if he had the mind to do so. The thought of him doing such a thing—planting a hard and powerful kiss to her lips—had her heart pounding in her chest. "And what exactly do you want from me?" she asked, hoping he was gentleman enough not to say what she was thinking.

"That morning you skipped out on me…I wasn't happy about it, especially when you agreed that we would spend a day and another night together."

His reminder sent a gush of heat flooding her cheeks. "You and I both know we probably said a lot of stuff that night we didn't mean," she said, suddenly feeling ill at ease with the memories.

"Aah…probably, but not about that," he said, his mouth quirking in dry humor. "You gave me your word and I was looking forward to more time with you."

She hadn't given her word…not exactly. She just hadn't done what she'd said she would do. "It was time for me to leave, Winston," she said, hoping he would see reason.

"No it wasn't and not like that. Not without the courtesy of letting me know you'd changed your mind. Not without even a goodbye."

Seriously, dude? Had you expected to come out of the shower to find me on the bed waiting for you, spread-eagle? She studied his features, saw the hard flint in the eyes staring her down and figured he probably had. Her mind began struggling for something to say since he was intent on being difficult, and a difficult bodyguard to Dr. R. J. Chambers was something she didn't need right now. To be quite honest, she'd rather not discuss this, but since he brought it up… "We didn't need a goodbye. You got what you wanted and I got what I wanted."

He shrugged. "Then call me greedy because I wanted more. And if I remember correctly, so did you at the time."

She could only stare at him thinking he was remembering correctly. She *had* wanted more. But that was before she'd come to her senses and realized more with him would only be asking for trouble. "I changed my mind. Get over it," she snapped.

"Easier said than done, Ainsley." He took a step back and let his eyes roam over her. She felt the heat of his gaze in places she wished she didn't.

Just when she thought she would combust from a simple look, he cocked his head to one side and said, "To get what you want, you'll need to give me what I want. What you owe me. I want a day and a night with you…with no interruptions."

"It won't happen."

"Is that your decision?" he asked.

"Yes."

"Your final decision? If you need more time to think—"

"I don't need any more time," she interrupted. "That's my final decision."

He nodded and shoved his hands into his pockets. "Then this is goodbye. And there's no need for me to mention your visit to Dr. Chambers."

Ainsley felt her stomach sink. He was letting her know he was playing hardball. He wouldn't give her what she wanted with Chambers, unless she slept with him again. Well, he could forget it. She didn't want the story that bad. But, she thought, with dread curling her stomach, she did want her job back. She needed her job back. There was nothing for her in Claxton and the sooner she could resume her life in New York, the better.

She nervously licked her lips while she held his gaze. Her mind taunted her. *He's such a good-looking man. Would sharing a bed again with him be so awful when you enjoyed it so much the first time?*

Yes, it would be awful. Having an affair of her own choosing was one thing; being coerced into one was another.

"Goodbye, Winston." She slid into the car and he closed the door while she snapped on her seat belt.

And then without saying anything else, she started the car and drove off, going back the way she came. She couldn't stop herself from looking through her rearview mirror at him. He was standing there, watching her leave.

It was only when he was no longer in sight that it occurred to her that he now had her full name, but the only thing she knew was his first name.

Chapter 7

Winston's hand wasn't quite steady as he took a drink and it was a drink he needed. Seeing Red again—or Ainsley since that was her name—had done him in. She had been the last person he'd expected to see when he'd left his lab to nab a trespasser.

And less than thirty minutes later he had let her go.

Watching her drive away had made him realize just how isolated it was out here. His godbrothers as well as Grady always joked about him being out on Barrett Shores alone. He always ignored their teasing because the seclusion had never bothered him…until today.

And what was that kiss about? A kiss he'd initiated that she'd returned with as much greed as he'd put into it. He liked stroking his tongue inside her mouth. Loved her taste. Loved the way she felt in his arms. And he was totally into her scent. He liked the way her flesh felt when he ran his tongue over her bottom lip. If he wasn't careful, she could become addictive.

Every muscle in his body suddenly went rigid. What the hell was wrong with him? No woman—and he meant *no* woman—got next to him or under his skin. And he'd be damned if he let her set a precedent. Three of his godbrothers had gotten whipped, and he'd sworn, along with Virgil and Zion, not to let it happen to them.

Winston smiled at the thought that he was up one on her. She had no idea that he was the very man she wanted to interview. He was Winston Coltrane, aka Dr. R. J. Chambers. He could have easily told her the truth, but had decided there was no way he would do so. After all, she was a reporter and they were known to spill any secrets a person might have.

And he had placed her between a rock and a hard place. She wanted a story and he wanted her. He hadn't realized just how much until he'd seen her again. And it was obvious his offer hadn't set too well with her. He had backed her against the proverbial wall and he had a feeling she wasn't one to be backed, no matter how badly she wanted a story. As far as he was concerned, he had every right to ask for more time with her. She had agreed to give him that and hadn't.

He reached into his pocket, pulled out her business card and looked at it. Plain, definitely not like her. There was nothing plain about Ainsley St. James at all. As far as he was concerned, she had looked just as hot today as she had that night. And so damn beautiful.

Suddenly a thought came into his mind and placing down his glass, he glanced over at Charley. "Need report on Ainsley St. James."

He heard the beeps and watched as lights on the board began flashing, which meant Charley was going furiously through data stored in his memory bank wired to the Google website. That was another bright idea of York's to aid with the research Winston did from time to time.

Charley interrupted his thoughts to ask, *"Male or female?"*

Winston raised his brow. There was a male? Were they related? Father and daughter perhaps? Curiosity had him saying, "Male."

"Male. Ainsley St. James. Born 1843 and died 1903. Founded Claxton, New Jersey. First mayor in 1870. Married Edna Boyd. Sons Edgar and Harry."

He'd heard enough. "Female."

"Female. Ainsley St. James. Age twenty-six. Former employer—The New York Times. *Candidate for mayor of Claxton, New Jersey. Lost."*

He sat up straight. Ainsley had a stint in politics? "When?"

"Repeat command. Failed communication."

He had to remember he wasn't talking to a human. "When did she lose the election?"

"Lost election in November. Two months ago."

Winston took a swallow of his drink and sat back in his chair. "Print report." This he had to read. "Good job, Charley. You keep it up and I'll hook you up with Siri."

Charley made a noise.

Winston chuckled. Seriously? Was that a grunt he heard? He wouldn't be surprised. At the time York had been creating Charley, he had been antifemale and had probably wired up Charley the same way. Personally, Winston liked hearing Siri's voice whenever he pulled out his iPhone.

He stood. He had dolphins to feed and pregnant turtles to track. The report on Ainsley would be there to read before he went to bed. Right now he wanted to put her out of his mind just like it seemed she had put him out of hers.

* * *

Ainsley entered her room at the resort and angrily threw down her purse on the first table she came to. She was fuming and the more she thought about Winston's proposition, the steamier she got. The nerve of the man!

Pushing open the French doors, she walked through them to stand on the balcony. She needed a breath of fresh air. It was a beautiful day but thanks to Winston whatever-his-name, she was in an ugly mood. The only way he would let her see Dr. Chambers was if they spent a day and night together? Uninterrupted? And what if after all of that Chambers still refused the interview? Winston would have gotten what he wanted and she would be left out to dry. Did she have the word *fool* tattooed on her forehead?

She cringed when her phone rang, hoping it wasn't Tessa or, even worse, Bobby. He'd already called her that morning to verify she would be making a trip to Barrett Shores to try and meet with Dr. Chambers. She hoped he wasn't calling back to find out how it went.

Walking into the living room, she pulled the phone out her purse, checked caller ID and cringed. It was Bobby. She started to ignore the call but figured he would only call back so she might as well talk to him now and get it over with.

She clicked on the phone. "Bobby?"

"You got good news for me, St. James?"

"Depends on how you look at it," she said, trying to make light of his question.

"Meaning?"

"Barrett Shores is private property. I did make it across the most god-awful bridge you could possibly imagine. You would not believe how rickety it looked. Like it was built in the early 1900s. It was made of wood and—"

"You're rambling. Did you or did you not get Chambers to agree to an interview?"

She paused, nibbled on her bottom lip a minute and then said, "Although I made it to Barrett Shores, I didn't get to see Chambers. I couldn't get past his bodyguard."

"His bodyguard? Come on, St. James. Surely you're not going to let one little bodyguard stop you from seeing an old man."

Ainsley rolled her eyes. "He's not exactly little, Bobby. In fact he's pretty big." Well-built, she thought to herself. She of all people should know since she had licked every inch of that well-built body one night.

"Then come up with a plan. I've already told Jones you're covering the story."

"What! Why did you do something like that?" Edwin Jones was Bobby's boss, the managing editor.

"Because I assumed you would be. Besides, I needed a bargaining chip when I asked him for your old job back. At first he bucked the idea, because like I said, your replacement has connections. But he's seen the reviews as well and agrees that something needs to be done. Getting a story on Chambers will give him the leverage he needs to go to Wendell to bring you back on."

Ainsley felt her gut tightening. Wendell was Jones's boss, the editor-in-chief. Jeez. Bobby had assumed she had the interview in the bag and that was so far from the truth it wasn't funny. She needed time to think, plan and execute.

"St. James?"

She drew in a deep breath. "Yes?"

"Is there something I need to worry about? You will get the scoop from Chambers, right? This is big news. They've already reserved a spot for Valentine's weekend. Our inside source says the FDA will approve Chambers's drug, so once he decides which pharmaceutical company he plans to marry, it will be front-page news and we want to have the scoop."

She drew in a deep breath, knowing now was the time to level with Bobby. But knew she could not do that. Too much was at stake and she had to come up with a plan.

"No, there isn't anything you need to worry about. I'll check in with you in a few days. Bye, Bobby." She quickly hung up the phone before he could question her about anything.

Placing the phone on the table, Ainsley moved back to the patio and stood at the rails and looked out at the ocean. The bottom line was that she had to come up with a plan.

The next day Winston leaned on the top railing of the huge tank that contained his sea horses. He watched them swim as they would in the ocean, upright, tails up, heads down. He'd always been fascinated by sea creatures so his family hadn't been surprised when he'd decided to pursue a career in marine biology. He'd decided on the University of Miami; after that he got both his grad and doctorate degrees from Cornell University.

When his parents had made the decision to move farther south to be close to his maternal grandparents, they'd left Barrett Shores to him with their blessings. He'd seized the perfect opportunity to resign from a job at a pharmaceutical company whose regulations, guidelines and policies were impeding all the things he felt he could accomplish. With his parents' approval, he had converted a part of his home into a sanctuary to further his studies on marine life.

Obviously his alias was no longer deterring those determined to find out his identity. At least for now Ainsley thought Winston and Chambers were different men. But her appearance yesterday meant it was just a matter of time before others showed up wanting the same thing she did—a story. He couldn't help but wonder who or what had tipped her off when he'd gone to great pains to build his false identity. In all honestly, it really didn't matter since he had no intention of granting her or anyone else an interview.

Before going to bed last night, he had read Charley's report on her and had found it rather interesting. For some reason she had made the decision to run for mayor of the town where she'd grown up. Given her great-great-great-grandfather founded the town and she was a hometown girl, she should have been a shoo-in and probably assumed that she was. Her rival, a relative newcomer to town, had obviously won over the good people and had even gone so far as to run a rather nasty campaign against her. The man claimed Ainsley had been a stripper at some New York nightclub while in college. Ainsley had denied the allegations and said she'd only been a dancer at the club. But in the small town a lot of the *good* people evidently thought a paid dancer was just as bad as a stripper and she had lost the election. Then it seemed her father had gotten hospitalized due to a heart attack the day after the election. Reports had speculated that the negative campaign against his daughter had been too much for the old man.

From all accounts, it seemed Ainsley wanted to return to the job at *The New York Times* that she had resigned from and figured he would be her first interview.

Like hell he would! No matter how good she'd been in bed—and she had been off the charts—nothing would make him change his mind.

What about that offer you made to her? About giving you a day and a night?

His thoughts burned deep in his mind. He'd only thrown that out there because he'd known she would refuse to do such a thing. And she had.

But what if she had agreed?

She hadn't and that was that. When they'd said their

goodbyes yesterday, they'd both known they were final. Neither of them intended to budge.

A few moments later he had washed up and was in the kitchen about to prepare lunch when Charley's security buzzer went off. *"Warning! Warning! Intruder!"*

Winston rubbed his hand down his face. For crying out loud, not another reporter. That was all he needed. "Scan perimeters, Charley."

"Vehicle left parked. South meadows. Oceanside."

That meant the person was on foot. Did the person actually assume they could scale the fence and not be seen? "Find and scan."

"Female. Same from twenty-four hours ago."

Winston frowned. Ainsley was back? "You sure?"

"Charley always sure."

Winston's frown deepened. Arrogant machine.

"Intruder scaling flagpole."

She was scaling the flagpole? This he had to see. "Display on monitor."

The screen flickered to life and within seconds he could see a curvy, feminine figure using her slender, lithe body to climb the flagpole. Damn. He felt his body get hard just watching her. She was more acrobatic than he'd imagined or remembered. She had worked that body of hers that night, but now he realized she had skills he hadn't even tapped into. Now he was beginning to wonder if perhaps she had been a stripper at one time like her mayoral opponent had claimed. Dressed in a black full-body leotard, she looked good with her legs wrapped around that pole, and a part of him wished they were wrapped around him instead.

He figured he had seen enough when she finally jumped down on other side of the fence and grabbed the duffel bag she'd tossed over earlier. On the other hand, he thought, maybe he hadn't seen enough when she started to strip off her leotard, down to her bra and panties.

"Notify authorities?" Charley barked out.

Winston's pulse rate escalated and heat surged through him. He found it hard to look away when she opened the duffel bag and pulled out a blouse and a pair of jeans and slid her curvaceous body into both.

"Notify authorities?" Charley asked again.

He wiped sweat from his brow. "No need," he said, pushing away from the kitchen counter. "She's about to be greeted by a welcome party of one."

"Repeat command. Didn't understand. Failed communication."

"No authorities." A smile touched his lips as he strode quickly to the nearest door.

Tucking her shirt into her jeans, Ainsley reached down to zip her duffel bag. Hopefully by the time she was detected she would have made her way to—

Her breath caught at the same time her heart leaped. She looked down at the hand clutching hers, and then raised her gaze to stare into the dark penetrating eyes she was getting to know so well. Where on earth had he come from?

"Back so soon? I was left with the impression after our conversation yesterday that you'd refused my offer. Glad to know you've reconsidered," he said.

"I have not!" she snapped, snatching her hand from his hold.

"Then you have five seconds to start telling me why you've trespassed on Barrett Shores again, or else I'm calling the police. You saw the sign at the bridge. You aren't welcome unless you're invited."

She crossed her arms over her chest. "How about letting Dr. Chambers speak for himself?"

"No."

"You're his bodyguard. Are you saying you're his spokesman, as well?"

He folded his arms over his chest and rocked back on his heels. "That's exactly what I'm saying. Now I'll be glad to escort you back to your car."

"I'm not going."

"Yes, you are. I would have come sooner to save you all the trouble, but I rather enjoyed watching you on that pole."

Winston smiled at the daggered looks she threw him. "I told you this place is secured. You should have known you would be seen." He paused and added, "And you handled that pole rather nicely, by the way. Had I known you had those skills, I would have ordered up a pole to my suite before you ran off that morning. There's nothing better than watching a sexy acrobatic woman in motion."

"Go to hell."

Suddenly, there was a loud roar of thunder. Winston tore his gaze away from Ainsley to stare up at the sky over the ocean. Damn. They were about to get one of those unexpected thunderstorms the area was known for this time of year. That meant the water under the bridge would be rising and it wouldn't be safe to cross it unless he got her to leave now.

He glanced back at her. Her attention had also been drawn to the ocean and the sky above it, taking in how dark it had suddenly gotten. "The weatherman said no chance of rain," she said accusingly, as if he had something to do with the weather.

He rolled his eyes. "You're a tourist. They're supposed to sell you on beautiful sunny days in January and not the ugly massive thundershowers we have on occasion."

He looked up at the sky again and shook his head. "Come on, you need to leave now so you can make it."

Her brows met in the middle of her forehead. "Make it where?"

"Back to Hilton Head. Once it starts raining the water rises under the bridge. Leaving at that point is dangerous and you'll be stuck here for a while."

Too late he realized he'd made a mistake in telling her that. He reached out to grab her and she darted out of his way and ran in the direction of the house, calling out over her shoulder, "Catch me if you can."

Growling with anger deep within his gut, he took off after her. She raced around in a lot of crazy circles but he was there, not too far away and right on her tail. And it was a tail worth being on, he thought when he lunged for her, forcing them both to fall in the sand. With a few quick moves he had her flat on her back with him over her.

"Get off me!"

"Not until I'm ready," he said staring down at her. For the umpteenth time he had to ask himself why she had to be a reporter. And one who was so damn beautiful.

"Get off me, Winston. I have sand all in my hair."

He chuckled. "I have news for you, there's sand all over you. That's what you get for running and trying to stall."

"Did it work?"

He frowned down at her. "No, you still have time to leave since it hasn't started raining yet."

And then, as if on cue, the entire sky fell open and huge raindrops pelted them. She laughed out loud as if pleased with the downpour. "It seems someone up there likes me, Winston."

He glared down at her and saw how the rain was washing her face at the same time it was pounding hard in his back. He stood and reached for her hand. "Come on. Hurry. Lightning this close to the ocean isn't a joke. We need to get up to the house."

She all but jumped for joy. "Yes, we need to get up to the house."

He held firm to her hand as they sprinted across the beach. When they finally reached the patio he pulled her under the rooftop, away from the pouring rain. "There's a shower house around the corner. We need to wash off all this sand before going inside."

Ainsley allowed herself to be led around the corner of the patio and she saw the enclosed shower he was talking about. It was bigger than her entire bathroom at home.

"You can use the shower first." Winston's voice interrupted her thoughts by saying, "Strip down. There're plenty of towels, shampoo, conditioner and everything you might need on that top shelf. There're also a few robes hanging up in there against the wall. When you're done, I'll take you inside for you to wash and dry your clothes."

She glanced inside the shower house and then glanced back at him suspiciously. "And just what are you going to be doing while I'm taking a shower?"

He smiled. "Enjoy looking at the rain while I wait my turn. Unless it's okay with you if we both saved time and water by showering together?"

Ainsley frowned thinking she could actually see the heat glaze his eyes from such a prospect. "No, it's not okay, so enjoy the rain and wait your turn."

She was about to open the door and step inside when she turned back to him. "I know your first name is Winston. What's your last name?"

He looked at her with deep consideration before saying, "Coltrane."

She lifted an arched brow. "Winston Coltrane?"

"Yes."

She smiled, nodded. "I like it." She then stepped inside the shower house and closed the door behind her.

Winston drew in a deep breath wondering if she was going to like the fact his alias was R. J. Chambers. Probably not, and he intended to keep that information from her as long as he could.

Chapter 8

Ainsley threw back her head and laughed as the water poured over her hair, face and all down her body. She wondered what kind of shampoo and body wash she was using. Whatever it was, it smelled good and left her hair feeling squeaky-clean.

"You do plan on getting out of there sometime today, right?"

She paused, almost forgetting he was out there. "Hey, be a good sport and wait your turn. This is fun."

She heard him chuckle over the spray of water. "Don't get to take showers much where you're from, huh?"

"Funny. I take showers all the time but I love this one. And what's the name of this shampoo and body wash? Both smell wonderful."

"It's called Misty Rain and the formula was created by a woman who used to live here years ago." Winston thought there was no reason to tell her the woman had been his grandmother. And that in addition to the shampoo and body wash, there was also soap and lotion, all with the same patented ingredients.

"I love it. As soon as I go to the store, I'm going to buy some."

"You can't," he said through the shower door. "It's not sold in any stores. Only online." There was also no need to tell her that since his brother had retired from the NFL, he'd set up shop on the west coast where all the Misty Rain products were produced.

"Okay, stand back. I'm coming out."

He wondered how she'd known he'd been right there by the shower door all this time. He stepped back and she opened the door wearing a huge white velour bath robe. She had tied the sash around her waist real tight but that didn't do any good since he'd already seen the body underneath.

She smiled then and he knew she was up to something. "While you're taking a shower you don't mind if I look around inside, do you?"

He frowned. "Yes, I do mind. Under no circumstances are you to bother Chambers. He lives and works in another part of the house and can't be disturbed. Doing so will put him in a bad mood and you wouldn't want that."

No, she didn't. The last thing she wanted was for Dr. Chambers to deny her an interview. "We didn't grab my duffel bag."

"Too late now. I'll go back for it when the rain stops."

He stepped inside the shower house and as soon as he did so, Ainsley quickly made her way toward the first door she saw. She wouldn't disturb the doctor; she would just let him know she was here. She reached out and tried opening the door and couldn't. It was locked.

"It's a good thing I locked all the doors, huh?"

Ainsley jerked around. Winston was standing in the middle of the shower door shamelessly naked and grinning at her. She stared, chewing the insides of her cheeks, grateful it wasn't her tongue. *Lordy.* She'd recalled him being built, but not *this* built. He hadn't been ashamed of showing his body that night and he wasn't ashamed of showing it now. Her gaze roamed all over him and came back to his middle each and every time. It was swollen. Hard. Fully erect.

"Ainsley?"

Licking her lips, she forced her eyes up when he called her name. "Yes?"

"Something told me you couldn't be trusted to do what you were told, so I locked all the doors."

She glared. "So what am I supposed to do while you're taking a shower?"

He chuckled. "Enjoy watching the rain."

He then closed the shower door, shutting off her view of him and his naked body.

Any hopes of Ainsley leaving anytime soon were dashed each and every time a lightning bolt rocketed across the sky, Winston thought, standing at the kitchen counter preparing sandwiches. He had made quick work of his shower after remembering how she had picked the lock to one of the gates yesterday.

"Will Dr. Chambers be joining us for lunch?" she asked him.

You wish. "No."

"Why not? He has to eat sometime."

"Yes, and he prefers eating alone and not with uninvited guests."

"I take it that means he knows I'm here."

Winston placed the sandwiches on a plate. "Yes, he knows. He was informed by Charley that we had an intruder the exact same time that I was."

She didn't say anything for a minute and then finally asked, "Dr. Chambers really is a recluse, isn't he?"

He shrugged. "Is that what you heard?"

"Yes. No one has ever met him and he's never been interviewed. But his studies on the use of sea creatures for medicinal purposes are well documented. I checked out one of his books from the library a few days ago."

"Did you?"

"Yes. I found his work fascinating. He's a brilliant scientist."

Winston tried not to let her compliment go to his head and said, "He prefers to be thought of as a biologist."

"There's a difference?"

"Technically no, but a biologist's duty is more clearly defined," he said, walking to the table with their sandwiches and placing the plate there. "A scientist mostly deals with natural or physical science, whereas biology is considered a natural science. A marine biologist studies organisms that live in salt water. You might want to remember that, if you ever get the chance to talk to Dr. Chambers. He has a pet peeve about being referred to as a scientist." He then turned to stroll over to the refrigerator for the lemonade.

"I can't wait until I meet Dr. Chambers."

Instead of opening the refrigerator, he turned and leaned against it. She sounded so sure of herself that he almost believed her. But he of all people knew the kind of meeting she was banking on was highly unlikely. He compressed his mouth as he watched Ainsley take a bite of the sandwich and lick her lips, his presence all but forgotten.

Too bad he couldn't say the same. She definitely looked out of place sitting at his kitchen table wearing a bathrobe. And he knew for a fact, there was nothing else under that robe. He had been there when she'd tossed all her clothing in the washer. And because they'd left behind her duffel bag, she was going to have to wait for her clothes to dry before she came out of that robe.

Out of that robe...

Now that was a thought he didn't wish to entertain. It wouldn't be so bad if he didn't know what she looked like, but because he did, he was having a hard time staying focused. Over the years he'd had his share of women, yet for the life of him, he didn't understand why she was different.

She was beautiful but then in his book all females were. But she had the kind of beauty that stood out. And she had a great body, which made for a deadly combination. He had been clobbered in the groin by both the first time he'd seen her walking into that nightclub. And last but not least, she knew how to use that body. He recalled touching her everywhere, tasting her everywhere. His tongue had moved all over the smooth skin on her face, lower to her shoulder blades, blazed a trail to her breasts and down past the indentation of her navel. It was then he'd become acquainted with her personal scent, and the moment he had absorbed it through his nostrils, he'd almost gone over the edge. And then when he'd tasted her between the legs, he'd been a goner.

"Hey, what's going on with that cold drink?"

Her words snapped him out of his reverie and he opened the refrigerator and retrieved a pitcher of lemonade. Grabbing a couple glasses as well, he walked back to the table and sat down. "You sound confident that you're going to meet the good doctor. Does that mean you've changed your mind about our deal?"

"I told you earlier that I have not."

Winston took a bite of his sandwich, trying like hell to downplay the effect sitting across from her was having on him. "Then nothing has changed. Why are you here, Ainsley? I hope you didn't think you could come back and change my mind. When Dr. Chambers is ready to let the world in on his life, then I'm sure that he will."

She put down her sandwich and he could tell she was trying to school her expression to hide her frustrations. "But why would he want to wait? Viagra took the world by storm and no man's life has been the same. If this new drug he's produced is bigger than Viagra, then we're talking about a massive explosion here. Once it's approved by the FDA, he'll be courted by every pharmaceutical company in the world. But first he'll need to sell the concept to them. If you recall, at first they were skeptical about something called a sexual enhancement drug."

He chuckled, seeing her angle...at least the one she wanted him to see. "And you think an interview will get people more comfortable with Norjamin?"

"Yes, and I'm sure once I talk to Dr.—"

"He's not to be disturbed. So eat your lunch. I'm hoping the rain stops so—"

"So I can leave?"

"Yes, so you can leave." And that was plainly and honestly put. He wasn't sure just how long his libido would last with her here. Her scent was getting to him again, and he was tempted to do something foolish—like admitting he was Dr. Chambers.

They continued eating in silence but a degree of uneasiness slid up his spine when, instead of slacking off, the rain started coming down in torrents. The roof was definitely taking a beating and he didn't want to think what was happening to the poor bridge.

As if she'd read his thoughts, she glanced out the window and keeping her tone light, she smiled and said, "Um, looks like you won't be getting rid of me any time soon, Winston."

Her words struck a discordant note with him. It was getting dark and if the rain didn't let up, it meant she would have to stay the night. He would rather she didn't. When it came to affairs, he believed in the B and M concept. Brief and meaningless.

"I wouldn't be all smiles about that if I were you," he said as his expression darkened. "The outside doors of this house have locks but there aren't any on the inner doors."

She fully faced him and stared him down. "Are you implying there's a chance you'd come into my room uninvited?"

Now it was his time to smile. "Um, I'm just saying."

Ainsley had no comeback and the room got quiet. Only the pounding rain was heard. In his mind it beat an erotic rhythm that started a throbbing sensation in his groin. He would love pounding into her the same way the rain was doing to the roof. The thought stirred his blood and had his chest heaving. He loved being intimate with a woman especially when it was raining. It somehow triggered primitive urges in him to mate.

"So, where's this Charley guy?" she finally asked, interrupting his thoughts. He glanced over at her and saw her wipe her mouth on the napkin and then take a sip of her drink.

"He's around," Winston said, shifting in his seat, feeling a tightening around his middle. And then after taking a sip of his own drink, he spoke up loudly. "Charley, someone wants to meet you."

She glanced around as if she expected some human to materialize from around the corner or from another room. He inwardly smiled when a section of his kitchen wall opened to reveal a panel board that was flashing. And when Charley replied, "Charley on duty," she covered her hand with her mouth in shock.

Smiling at Ainsley, Winston said, "He trying to tell you in a nice way he can't socialize while he's working."

Once the shock wore off, Ainsley began laughing and couldn't seem to stop.

"You find something funny?" Winston broke in to ask her.

She shook her head, wiped the tears from her eyes as her laughter slowly began subsiding. "Sorry, but Charley's not a man."

Leaning over the table, Winston whispered, "Better not say that too loud. He has a thing for Siri."

Ainsley raised a brow. "The iPhone announcer?"

"One and the same."

That made Ainsley start laughing again and she concluded she needed the laugh because everything that had happened today had been downright silly. First, her thinking she could use her expertise and skill as a pole dancer to scale that flagpole. It worked but she hadn't gotten across the fence undetected. And just to think, it wasn't a man but a machine who'd ratted on her.

"So what all can Charley do?"

Winston's voice sank lower when he said, "Whatever he can do, I can do better."

She rolled her eyes. "We're talking about in the way of security, right?" Did he have to look so striking sitting across from her in a bathrobe? This entire thing was strange at best. Why was he still wearing one? She was waiting for her clothes to dry but what was his excuse? The only conclusion she could reach was that he didn't intend to let her out of his sight for one minute. Not even for the time it took to put on clothes.

"In that case there's none that can compare. Charley's state-of-the-art and the brainchild of one of my friends who own a security company in New York," he interrupted her thoughts to say.

"Charley's cute." And she figured he was wondering

how she knew that. "I like a man with a lot of buttons that I can push."

Winston chuckled. "He thinks you're cute, too, and he enjoyed seeing you earlier in your bra and panties."

The smile was quickly wiped from her face. "He saw me in the shower before I undressed?"

"No, he saw you, like I did, when you did that pole and stripped down afterward to put on your jeans and top. Charley got a thrill but it wasn't anything I hadn't seen before. In fact, I saw a lot more skin that night. Tasted it, too."

She glared at him. "Glad you recall that episode because it won't happen again."

His smile widened. "And that's where our thought processes differ because I'm going to try like hell to make sure it does happen again, Ainsley."

Deciding not to waste time going back and forth with him on an issue that was dead in the water, she said, "Since we have time to kill, you want to show me around while my clothes are drying?"

"I'd rather not."

She shrugged. "Then suit yourself. We can just sit here and enjoy the rain."

That sounded doable, Ainsley thought, if he wasn't sitting there staring at her. It reminded her too much of the night they'd met and how he had ogled her then. The memories were causing goose bumps to form on her skin. No matter how she tried forgetting that night, she couldn't.

"Too bad it hadn't been raining that night we met," he broke the silence to say.

Bewildered by his statement, she asked, "Why?"

He held her gaze when he replied. "I like making love to the sound of the rain. It does something to me each and every time. Makes me think of hot and wild sex."

She swallowed, thinking that he was deliberately trying

to get next to her and she refused to let him…although blood was rushing through her veins even now. His closeness was having an effect on her; she couldn't and wouldn't deny that. And he smelled good. Like man and rain. The scent of that body wash and shampoo clung to their bodies, but mingled with his natural aroma, it smelled differently. Like that of a robust man whose bones were made for jumping.

She tightened her hand on her glass thinking, at that moment, she needed something a lot stronger than lemonade. But first, she needed to get them out of this kitchen. It was huge but still intimate. "If you don't want to show me around, then tell me more about Charley. What else can he do?"

"Can't tell you."

"Can't or won't?"

"Both, I imagine," he drawled in a Southern accent she found way too sexy. He looked at her from beneath long, silky lashes and said in a low husky tone, "But there is a section of the estate I can show you."

Ainsley felt her blood stir. "Which is?"

"Guest quarters. If this weather keeps up it will be impossible for you to leave before morning."

For some reason the thought of sleeping under the same roof as him didn't bother her. Maybe it should since she could feel that annoying ripple of attraction between them. Even now their gazes were hanging on to each other and there was no denying the currents of electricity in the air that had nothing to do with the storm roaring outside. "So…" she said, placing down her glass. "Can I trust you to do the right thing?"

"Not entirely," he said in a velvety smooth voice, one that sent desire oozing up her spine. "If given the chance, I'll have you naked in a heartbeat."

"At least you're honest." She broke eye contact with him

and looked out the window where she could see the ocean. Winston was a complication she didn't need, and she figured they needed to change the subject and fast. "Even with all this bad weather, it's beautiful here," she said and meant it.

"It is. There's nothing like making love on the beach."

So much for changing the subject. She glanced back at him and felt desire ripple through her again. He was intentionally taunting her, making her lose focus, get too relaxed. She absently ran her fingers through her still-damp hair. She could just imagine how it looked. "I need to do something with this," she said.

"Not really. I like you looking wild."

She chuckled. "And crazy?"

He shook his head and glanced at her hair. "No, just wild. Just like you were that night."

Yes, she was. But why was he making her remember?

"You even clawed up my back pretty damn good," he added.

She frowned. "Hey, what about all those passion marks you put on me?"

There appeared a satisfied gleam in his eyes. "They're all gone now. Want some more?"

His tone held a suggestive edge, one that was too dangerous to her peace of mind right now. "No thanks."

Her eyes then narrowed on him, knowing it was time to set him straight. She was tired of his game-playing. "Look, I didn't come here for this."

He narrowed his gaze right back. "I know why you came, when I distinctly told you Chambers would not be doing an interview…unless you agreed to my terms. You didn't and that should have been the end of it. But you're back, so evidently that wasn't the end. If you assume you can get me to change my mind then you're wrong. I don't act on emotions, I act on desires and at the moment I desire you to the point where I could probably eat you alive. I probably won't be physically sated until I make love to you so hard you scream my name."

Ainsley drew in a swift breath. His voice had an abrasive edge to it and she had a feeling he meant everything he'd said. Reading between the lines she couldn't help but conclude that she'd been nothing more to him than a bed partner and, if they made out again, that's all she ever would be. That's how he dealt. He was not into lasting relationships, just physical ones. And right now he desired something physical with her and she had a feeling it would be even more explosive than the last time.

She couldn't help wondering about the identity of the woman who had broken his heart and tossed him out. And there had been a woman, she was certain of it. A woman he had trusted and loved. She had hurt him, left him bitter, full of anger. He hadn't let go and, until he did, he would never fully belong to any woman.

She knew the feeling because she doubted if she could ever fully belong to any man. There was no man to blame; it just wasn't in her makeup. She dated when it pleased her and gave her heart to no man. Sex had always been an afterthought because there had never been a time she knew she couldn't do without it. There had never been anything earth-shattering about any of her bed partners...until that one night with Winston.

And she knew that was the reason she had hauled ass that morning he'd been in the shower and why she was fighting a repeat performance with him now. She had felt things when he'd been inside her that she hadn't ever felt before. And the thought that making love to a man could push her over the edge was scary.

And that's why she knew she couldn't let him touch her again that way. She would not only lose her mind, she would be at a risk of losing her soul, and then the loss of her heart would surely follow.

"So why don't you put us both out of our misery, Ainsley? Let's make love all over this damn place," he said in a deep, husky voice that was more than tempting. It was downright lethal.

She met his gaze thinking it never ceased to amaze her how some men operated. Going between a woman's legs was just that…going between a woman's legs. Not love. Not a desire to commit. No strings attached.

"Who says I'm in misery?" she asked, trying not to get unnerved by him.

"I say so. And I intend to take you out of it."

And the next thing she knew he was out of his chair—nearly knocking it over in the process—moving around to her side of the table and pulling her into his arms.

She tried to protest but he kissed her into silence.

Chapter 9

Ainsley tried resisting but only for a little while, less than a couple seconds to be exact. Winston knew the moment he'd broken through her resistance. That was all the time it took to ease his tongue between her parted lips and sweep her into sweet surrender.

And it was definitely sweet. Her senses had gotten torched like his and she was returning his kiss, mating with his tongue, and opening her mouth wider to consume and be consumed. She was his for the taking and he was doing a damn good job of it.

There was something so profoundly sensual about kissing her. He had enjoyed it that night and he was enjoying it now. Already, his lower body was throbbing beneath his bathrobe, screaming for release and pushing him to indulge even more. And then there was the provocative scent of her, jostling his senses all over the place and taunting him to be greedier. Even after her shower when the smell of Misty Rain should be entrenched into her skin, he could still pick out her natural scent and it was stirring up intense desire within him.

He lowered his hands to her waist to ease open the sash to her robe, needing to touch her bare skin. His hands traced a path over her breasts, spanned her small waist and caressed her shapely hips. She tried pulling away her mouth, but he took possession and locked his down on hers, feasting more greedily, and he knew he'd won her over when she began moaning and returning the kiss in equal measure.

Winston moved his thigh between her legs and felt her heated skin on his flesh. All the while he'd been sitting across from her, he had imagined touching her this way, tasting her, making love to her again.

He slowly pulled back his mouth. "I love the feel of your sex on my thigh. All it will take is for you to open yourself a little and I can ease inside," he murmured, trailing heated kisses along the corner of her mouth and down the side of her neck.

To really push her over the edge, he moved his hand lower to touch her intimately and moaned when he found her wet. There was nothing like the scent of an aroused woman and hers flowed through his nostrils, clung to his membranes. She moaned and leaned closer to him, letting him know she liked the feel of his fingers inside of her. He studied her features, saw the intensity in the gaze staring back at him, the beauty of her, and a deep hunger erupted within him. He knew at that moment he could eat her alive.

"Do you know what I like even more than your aroused scent?" he whispered close to her ear.

"No," she said in a tortured moan. "What?"

"Your taste." He dropped to his knees and before she could push him away, his mouth latched onto her sex. The moment his tongue invaded her he remembered why he'd wanted to do this again. Why he enjoyed going down on her. Her taste was so delicious it was almost addicting.

He was finding out the hard way that Ainsley St. James was an irresistible morsel he couldn't get enough of.

Ainsley knew she was a goner at the first flicker of his tongue. "Oh, yes!"

She bracketed his head with her hands and swallowed the tightening lump in her throat when his tongue went deeper, feasting on her like she was an after-dinner dessert.

"Oh, my," she moaned when she saw what he intended to do. Lick her right into a climax. And he wasn't wasting precious time doing so. She first felt the intense stirring in her bones followed by a rush of blood through her veins. The orgasm ripped through her and her thighs began to tremble. He tightened his hands on her hips, licking harder followed by gentle nipping sensations from his teeth.

At that moment she felt as if everything inside her had been waiting just for this moment, the first move by him to remind her of what it had been like before. He kept going with long, leisurely strokes taking her orgasm to an unimaginable level.

She slowly began winding down, feeling drained and sapped, as if she was having a serious meltdown. With no strength left, she sagged against him, clung tightly to his shoulders as he absorbed her tremors with his mouth.

And when her thighs stopped quivering, he released her and pressed his face against her stomach. He placed a light kiss right under her belly button before leaning back to gaze up at her. His lips were still wet from her juices. All she could do was stare at him. At that moment she was assaulted by all types of emotions. What had started out almost a week and a half ago as impersonal sex between two individuals was beginning to get personal and she didn't know how to stop it.

"You enjoyed that?" he asked quietly, breaking the silence between them.

All she could do was nod, but that was enough to elicit the smile that touched his lips. Standing, he picked her up in his arms to carry her over to the counter and sit her on it. Then he kissed her, soothing her soft moans and letting her taste herself on his tongue. And she knew at that moment that, although Winston had an aversion to ever letting a woman dig her claws into him, he was an unselfish lover. The kind any woman would want and for her everything other men before him had never been.

Ending the kiss, he pulled back slightly and whispered against her moist lips, "I love giving you pleasure."

She didn't doubt that, if the last time and today was anything to go by. After drawing in a deep breath she exhaled, fanning the dark hairs matting his chest. She finally found the strength to lift her head and look into the penetrating eyes that ensnared hers. There was no regret there and she knew he wouldn't find it in her eyes. He'd scored another point if his purpose had been to prove one. Yet she'd gotten something out of this, as well. And since she was the one who'd come unglued, she could even say she'd gotten more than he had. He had given her pleasure but had held back his own. Why?

Even now from the feel of his erection pressing against her leg she knew he was powerfully aroused. Why didn't he take full advantage when he had the chance?

As if he read the question in her eyes, he took his finger and placed it under her chin and said huskily, "The next time I go inside you will be because I know you want me there, and not because I've gotten there through any type of underhanded seduction on my part."

She didn't have to wonder what he was talking about. The mere fact that she was sitting in his kitchen naked proved the intensity of her desire for him. They had proven before that sex between them wasn't just good, it was off the charts. They had the ability to share unadulterated sexual pleasure. She couldn't deny that even if she tried.

He reached out and stood her on the floor. "Your clothes should be dry now," he said huskily, his hands reaching out and cupping her breasts as if he appreciated their fullness. "Get dressed and meet me back here in five minutes."

He dropped his hands to his side and added in a serious tone, "I'm going upstairs to get dressed and I trust that you won't take it upon yourself to wander about. Any area beyond the kitchen and laundry room is off-limits. I wouldn't advise you to seek out Chambers and disturb him from his work. You'll only get on his bad side and, in the end, he'll refuse to see you, no matter what I say."

She watched him go, feeling the nipples of her breasts ache. When he was no longer in sight, she sighed deeply. She couldn't believe what had happened in this kitchen. No, she corrected herself. She *could* believe. The man had a way with his fingers and mouth.

And he had a way with her.

He should not have tasted her again, Winston thought as he pulled a T-shirt over his head. Now he wouldn't be getting a lick of sleep for sure tonight.

Lick...

Sensual shivers went through him as he remembered. It was as if his tongue was meant to go inside her somewhere, whether it was in her mouth or between her legs. He might as well brand it with a big, whopping A.

He finished dressing, listening to the storm still raging outside. But that was nothing compared to the storm raging inside him. Now he would be walking around with a hard-on for no telling how long. He should have known better, but going down on her had been as natural as breathing.

And that wasn't good. She could become an addiction. A weakness. A woman he thought he couldn't do without. And that was unacceptable. Already whenever he saw her, he thought of sex, was constantly hard. Ready. And for a man who could get so involved with his work that he could put sex on the back burner for months before thinking about it, that wasn't good.

He decided it would be best for all concerned if he kept his distance from her for the rest of her stay here. With all the rain he wouldn't risk sending her across the bridge and he wouldn't risk taking her back by boat, either.

But first thing in the morning he intended to see her off with a stiff warning. If she returned for whatever reason, he wouldn't hesitate calling the authorities.

Shivers ran all over Ainsley as she slid into her dry jeans. She pushed back several strands of hair from her face and wished she had a band to put it in a ponytail. *Hey, forget the band for your hair. What you need is a damn lock to your cookie jar.*

She took a deep breath and then slowly inhaled knowing that was so true. She could have stopped him the minute he'd dropped to his knees with a sharp slap to his face. Instead, what did she do? Grabbed ahold of his head and all but shoved her cookie down his throat. And he had eaten it up. Literally.

Ainsley rubbed a hand along her face, purely disgusted with herself. Although he didn't get any further than going down on her, he really should not have made it that far. She should have done something.

Oh, but she had.

She had moaned out her enjoyment and would have even

been ready to return the favor with no arm-twisting. Both mortified and irritated, she put on her blouse and tucked it into her jeans. He had set her up, knowing all along how things would end. Right now he was probably pleased with himself.

Dressed, she leaned against the wall trying to fight back the sensations still thrumming through her body, especially there…between her legs. His mouth had triggered all kind of primal urges with the first brush of his tongue. And then there was the way he had cupped her breasts as if he'd every right to do so. She hadn't protested then, either. It didn't make sense how a man she'd met no more than two weeks ago could elicit that much desire within her.

Deciding she wanted to forget what happened and hoped he did as well, she glanced around. Even the laundry room off the kitchen was impressive. She saw another door and wondered where it led and was tempted to go find out. Then she remembered Winston's warning. The last thing she wanted was to get on Dr. Chambers's bad side and ruin things with him before she got a chance to officially meet him and plead her case for an interview.

Ainsley glanced out the window and saw it was still storming. There was no doubt in her mind that tomorrow morning Winston intended to ask her to leave, which meant she had to come up with a plan and fast. Chambers was here on the grounds somewhere, and she needed to find out where. This place was huge and he could be just about anywhere. She wondered…

Moving quickly to the kitchen she headed straight to the wall where the security panel was located. Checking over her shoulders to make sure Winston wasn't lurking around, she edged closer. As if the security system sensed her presence, lights on the panel board began blinking.

After swallowing, Ainsley said, "Charley, where's Dr. Chambers."

More lights began blinking. *"Repeat command. Failed communication."*

She let out a disgusted sigh. She didn't have much time before Winston returned, breathing down her neck again and there was no doubt in her mind he would watch her like a hawk for the rest of the evening. That meant she needed to at least know in what part of the house the doctor was working. Winston had to sleep sometime and when he did she would make her move. She hated having to disturb Dr. Chambers, but according to what she'd read in one of his books, he did just as much work at night as he did in the day. A lot of the sea animals he was studying were creatures of the night.

Deciding to take another approach, she asked. "Where's the lab?"

"Basement floor, east wing."

She nodded. At least she'd gotten that much information, although she wasn't sure where the east wing was. But she was determined to find it.

"Fascinated by Charley I see."

Ainsley quickly swung around hoping she didn't have a guilty look on her face. And she tried not to make it obvious she was checking out Winston. He had changed into another pair of jeans and a blue T-shirt. Heat immediately surged through her and she fought it back. He looked good but deep down she knew there was more to Winston Coltrane than the clothes he wore.

He was definitely a complex man. Complex and fascinating at the same time. And she would round it off with bold. She had a feeling he did whatever the hell he felt like and answered to no one. What other man would seduce a woman in the kitchen of his employer's home, actually go down on her when someone might walk in on them at any minute? But then, didn't that make her just as bold as him?

"Come on, time to feed the dolphins," he said.

"Dolphins?"

"Yes."

She glanced out the window. "In case you've forgotten, it's storming and—"

"The dolphin tank is on the back in an enclosed area."

"Oh."

Already he was walking away toward the laundry room and opening that door that she'd been curious about earlier. She quickly followed, determined not to be left behind. As soon as she walked through the doorway she saw the stairs that led down to what seemed to be a basement area.

He stood aside. "After you."

She nodded and began walking down the stairs. She shook her head at just how trusting she was of this man she really didn't know. Other than knowing his name was Winston Coltrane and he was a bodyguard to Dr. R. J. Chambers, she didn't really know a lot about him. She hadn't found it necessary to ask for a full disclosure of his life the night they'd spent together. All she knew at the time was that the man had set her stomach fluttering the moment she'd laid eyes on him and the sexual chemistry flowing between them had been strong. But still, he was taking her down some stairs that could lead to heaven knows where, so she decided she needed to know more about him.

"So why would a bodyguard feed dolphins? Is that part of your duties?" she asked over her shoulder.

"It is if you have a degree in marine biology."

She almost missed the next step and he quickly reached out to grab her by the waist to keep her from falling. "Thanks, you can let go of me now."

"You sure?"

"Positive."

He slowly removed his hand and she felt the withdrawal of his touch in every part of her body. She frowned up at him. "You never told me that," she said in an accusing voice.

Stifling a grin, he said, "Never told you what?"

"That you were anything to Dr. Chambers other than his bodyguard. You're also his assistant, aren't you?"

He hunched his shoulders. "Possibly."

"You are, so go ahead and admit it. Otherwise why would you be feeding dolphins?"

He smiled. "Because they're hungry. Now stop asking questions and let's move on. We're almost an hour late and Lucy and Ricky don't like late meals."

"Lucy and Ricky?"

"Yes."

She chuckled. "Oh, that's cute. Who named them?" she asked as they began making their way down the stairs again.

"Dr. Chambers."

"That figures." And then she decided to ask. "Do you think Dr. Chambers will come down while we're here?"

"I doubt it. He has more important things to do. A full moon is expected in a few days and he wants everything to be ready."

They had reached the bottom floor and he came to stand beside her. "Ready for what?"

"Mating of the sea horses. But before there's mating, there's a few days where they go through this courtship ritual."

A huge smile touched her lips. "You're kidding, right?"

"No, I kid you not," he said, grabbing hold of her elbow to lead her toward an area where she could see a huge tank ahead.

She tried ignoring the stirrings in her stomach from his

touch. "You mean sea horses actually court before they mate?"

"Yes. As far as I'm concerned that's too much time wasted. I say just get the one you want and do your thing."

Like he'd done to her. Like she'd done to him. "Um, I sort of like the courtship part."

"I'm sure most women would."

Was that disdain she heard in his voice? She wouldn't be surprised if it was. "There's nothing's wrong with a man making a woman feel special before he *does* her."

He chuckled. "If he works it right, he can make her feel special while he's *doing* her. Kill two birds with one stone, so to speak."

Ainsley stopped walking, which made him have to stop, too. "May I ask you something?"

A smile touched his lips. "Ask away. That doesn't mean I'll answer."

She pushed a hand through her hair. If she was a violent person, she would hit him—just like had she been in her right mind, she would have slapped him right before he'd gone down on her. "Your mother."

Lifting a brow, he asked, "What about her?"

"You know her?"

He chuckled. "Of course I know her. She and my father have been happily married for close to thirty-eight years. They were married a few years before I was born. I'm the oldest."

She nodded. "You have siblings?"

Winston wondered where her line of questioning was headed but decided to answer anyway. "Yes, a brother who is three years younger."

"No sisters?"

"No."

Nodding again, she asked, "Are you and your mother close?"

She looked so serious, he thought, studying her features. Her eyes, full of questions, were a beautiful shade of brown. He'd thought that the first night they met and thought it now. And her lips were erotically shaped in a way that would make a man want to ply them with kisses all day. He could see himself nibbling the corners and then taking his tongue and laving the center before finally wiggling that same tongue inside for a feast.

"Winston?"

"Yes?" he said, moving his gaze from her lips back up to her eyes.

"Are you and your mother close?"

Why did he always feel this burning awareness in the pit of his stomach whenever he gazed into her eyes for so long? "Yes, we're close. Why?"

She shrugged. "Just trying to figure something out," she said as she began walking again.

He joined in step beside her. "Figure out what?"

"What you have against women."

He stopped walking and she stopped, as well. She could see the deep frown etched in the grooves of his face. "I have nothing against women. In fact I enjoy women."

She placed her hand on his arm and tilted her head to the side as if to assure herself that she had his undivided attention when she said, "Yes, you *enjoy* women, but you'll never love one."

The nerve endings in his arm began to come alive at her touch. That wouldn't be so bad if her scent wasn't surrounding him as well, making his pulse rate escalate. He tried focusing on what she'd said and would be honest with her like he was with all women—especially any with foolish romantic notions.

"You're right. I'll never love one."

He decided that with her he would go a little further by saying, "But it has nothing to do with any lack of respect for women. I operate on the ideology that once burned you have the good sense not to play with fire again." And that was the bottom-line truth of the matter. Unlike his godbrother Virgil who believed in "do them before they do you," he preferred to enjoy the opposite sex and let them know up-front what would or would not happen between them. Then you wouldn't have to worry about things getting crazy later.

They began walking again. "It's hard to believe some woman broke your heart."

Winston wondered why they were discussing this. She'd asked her question and he had answered it. Why wasn't it the end of story? "It happens even to the best of men," he heard himself saying when he probably just should have kept his mouth shut. "I was young, stupid and figured one day I would meet a woman and share the same kind of marriage my parents had."

"What happened?"

He opened his mouth to tell her it wasn't her business and then decided maybe she needed to know in order to understand just how serious he was about *not* falling in love. "She betrayed me."

He heard her surprised gasp. "With another man?"

"Yes." He cocked his head and glanced over at her and saw the shocked look on her face. "You act like you find that hard to believe."

"I do. You aren't exactly chopped liver."

He smiled. The woman was good for his ego. "Well, she did. I didn't need anyone in my life that I couldn't trust."

She didn't say anything and it was just as well, he thought. He'd probably given her too much information anyway, but talking to her took his mind off making love to her. And he had been thinking about it; thinking about it a lot even though he tried not to. He wanted her. Spending any amount of time with her triggered his libido like crazy. He couldn't wait for tomorrow morning to get here so she could leave. Hell, if it stopped raining long enough, he'd even be tempted to take her back over to Hilton Head on his boat this evening.

When they got closer to the tank she rushed on ahead when she saw the two dolphins bobbing on the surface of the water. "Oh, Winston, they are beautiful."

"Thanks." When he saw her smile at Lucy and Ricky, a weird feeling of satisfaction raced through him.

"Okay, which is which?"

"This is Ricky," he said touching the nose of the dolphin closer to them. "And the other one is Lucy. She's sort of shy."

"How can you tell them apart?"

"I've worked with them long enough to know them. But to tell a male from a female you look at the slits on their belly. The male has—"

"Aah, I get the picture." A deep blush covered her cheeks.

"I can't believe talking about animals' reproductive organs makes you blush."

"Well, it does."

"Then it's a good thing you won't be here when the sea horses start mating. They can get downright nasty. They like doing it until he gets pregnant."

She jerked her gaze from the dolphins to him. "He?"

A smile curved his lips. "Yes, in sea horses it's the male who gets pregnant."

Ainsley started laughing and couldn't stop. Winston lifted a brow and stared at her. "You find that amusing?"

She smiled at him sweetly once her laughter subsided. "Yes, it's good to know there is justice somewhere in the world after all."

Chapter 10

Seated at the same table she'd sat at earlier for lunch, Ainsley watched Winston move around the kitchen preparing dinner. She had offered to help but he'd declined her assistance. He didn't have to turn her down twice. She wasn't a woman who liked being in the kitchen, anyway. Takeout worked just fine for her. Besides, the more distance between her and Winston the better. Watching his interactions with the dolphins had gotten her mind off him for a little while. But now he was back to holding court and taking possession of her thoughts.

There was a strong tug on certain parts of her body when she remembered him in this very kitchen earlier that day with his head between her legs. At the time all his attention had been focused on her and giving her pleasure. And he had. Now his attention was on preparing the food and with the same single-minded concentration. Her entire body was buzzing with a degree of desire that she hadn't known was possible until she'd met him.

"Lucy and Ricky like you."

Ainsley smiled at the significance of that and appreciated him breaking into her thoughts before he short-circuited her brain.

"And I like them." And she'd said that with all honesty. She rarely got taken with sea animals, but she'd been taken with that pair. It was amazing how well they were able to understand Winston's orders. After making sure they were fed, he had proceeded to get them to do various tricks.

The closest she'd gotten to dolphins had been when she and her parents had been lucky enough to sit in the front row at SeaWorld one year. Today she'd not only been closer but had even petted the sea creatures.

Winston had been wonderful with them. She wondered if Dr. Chambers realized how fortunate he was to have him for an assistant.

She leaned back in her chair and took a sip of her tea as she continued to watch him move. His muscular thighs filled out the well-worn jeans and his hard muscles rippled beneath his shirt. The man had such an amazing body, every time she focused on it she could feel heat suffuse her pores.

She couldn't help but recall what he'd shared with her about the woman who had betrayed him. She'd got the feeling he hadn't intended to, but he had and a part of her couldn't imagine any woman in her right mind doing something like that to him. Now she understood why he worked so hard not to let down his guard, a guard he had deliberately put up between them. The only time he'd let it down was when sexual tension had been too overwhelming.

The rain had finally stopped an hour ago, and she'd fully expected him to suggest that she leave, but so far he hadn't. So now she had her plans in place. Charley had revealed the location of the lab and she intended to try her luck in finding it once she was certain Winston had gone to sleep.

It would be a risky move but one she didn't have any other choice but to make. There was no way she was leaving tomorrow before seeing Dr. Chambers, whether Winston wanted her to or not.

"You're going to have to stay the night."

His words intruded on her thoughts and she inwardly released a sigh. "It's stopped raining. I probably can make it across the bridge," she said, figuring she needed to present some semblance of protest.

"I wouldn't try it if I were you. It's gotten dark and going across the bridge after a pouring rain can be dangerous. I suggest you wait until morning. I can put you up for the night. There's plenty of room here."

That was an understatement, especially since it seemed Dr. Chambers lived in another part of the house. That prompted her to ask, "Will Dr. Chambers be joining us for dinner?"

"No," he replied as he took a pan out of the oven.

"He has to eat sometime."

"And he will. I'm preparing enough, but he prefers his privacy."

She didn't say anything for a minute and then asked, "Does he know I'm still here?"

There was a soft chuckle. "Oh, trust me, he knows."

Ainsley picked up her cup of tea, not sure if that was a good thing or a bad thing. "Then why hasn't he made an appearance and said hello?"

"Why should he? You've shown up twice now. Uninvited."

She sighed, knowing there was no way she could deny that. "At least he knows I'm persistent." She took a sip of her tea. "Hey, this is pretty good."

"Thanks. Dinner will be ready in a second if you want to go ahead and wash up."

She nodded, took another sip of her tea before standing. "Will I get to see any other parts of the house? You're keeping me confined to the kitchen and laundry area."

He shrugged broad shoulders while he opened the refrigerator. "You'll get to see the guest room where you'll be staying. That's about it. No reason for you to see more."

She tried not to show her irritation as she headed toward the laundry room where a powder room was located. She knew he was serious and wouldn't be giving her a tour. That meant she would have to find her way to the lab on her own.

Winston watched her leave and his dark eyes narrowed as he watched the sway of her hips in her jeans. The woman had more curves than she knew what to do with. He shook his head, remembering their night together and knew she did know what to do with them, which was why he wanted her back in his bed again.

He swore under his breath thinking morning couldn't come quick enough to suit him. The woman all but had him tied in knots. First, he'd been surprised by her reaction to Lucy and Ricky. She actually liked them. Most women—the few women he had invited here—would almost die of fright and acted as if the animals would eat them alive if they got too close. Not Ainsley. She had petted them, talked to them and had even helped feed them. He meant what he'd told her. Lucy and Ricky liked her and they didn't take to everyone. Smart mammals.

He carried the platter and bowls over to the table. Like he'd told her, she was an uninvited guest and he would be in his right to let her eat alone. However, he couldn't do that any more now than he could do it at lunch. But still, already she had cost him an entire day of work, which meant while she slept tonight, he would make up the day by working in the lab.

He heard her returning. After dinner, once he had her settled in the guest room and out of his way and sight, he could get some semblance of normalcy back in his life by drowning his thoughts in his work.

Three hours later Ainsley paced the guest room Winston had given her. Just as she'd assumed it would be, it was simply beautiful. The one large window in the room afforded her a gorgeous view of the ocean, and even at night she could see the waters underneath a moon-kissed sky.

The meal he'd prepared, low-country stew over rice with mouthwatering corn bread, had been delicious. He'd credited his cooking skills to his mother and paternal grandmother. Over dinner she had tried picking information out of him about the lab and was fairly certain he hadn't detected her ulterior motive for doing so. Now at least she had a good idea of where she needed to go after leaving this guest room to find the lab. And she'd all but gotten Winston's affirmation that Dr. Chambers would be working late tonight.

During dinner she had pretended she could barely keep her eyes open, and afterward he had escorted her up a flight of stairs where several spacious bedrooms were located.

So now she was waiting, giving Winston time to settle in for the night and go to sleep in his bedroom, a floor above her. He had knocked on her door an hour or so ago with an oversize T-shirt for her to sleep in. The shirt was thrown across the bed for her to put on later. Right now her main objective was seeing Dr. Chambers.

What if he refused to see her? What if he sounded the alarm and ordered Winston to put her out? That meant she would have to sleep in her car. That also meant she would have lost her one and only chance for that interview.

Ainsley glanced over at the clock and saw it was close to midnight. The house was completely quiet and she figured now was time to make her move. She tiptoed to the door and opened it to peek out. All was quiet and dark except for a night-light that lit the hallway. Easing the door shut behind her, she walked quietly to the staircase and instead of going up another level, she took the stairs down to the first floor. Since Winston had told her the guest rooms were on the west side of the house, she knew she had to go to the opposite side to find Chambers's lab. Thanks to Charley she knew it was in the basement in the east wing.

Once she made it to the main floor, she crossed the huge living room, went past the kitchen and laundry area. Her goal was that door they'd gone through earlier to feed the dolphins. Moments later, she stood in front of it. What if an alarm sounded when she opened it?

Ainsley drew in a deep breath knowing she had to take her chances. She reached for the doorknob and turned it slowly. When the door opened without a sound, she released the breath she hadn't known she was holding until now. Looking over her shoulder to make sure all was still quiet, she moved down the stairs.

Winston's erection began throbbing the minute he heard the steady and determined footsteps coming down the stairs. He couldn't help but appreciate Ainsley's tenacity.

He had known what her plans for tonight were when she had pretended total exhaustion at dinner. He had found her playacting rather amusing to say the least. More than once he had stared across the table at her, struggling not to allow her fake drowsiness to become a total turn-on. But there had been something about her lowered lashes and flushed cheeks that had made him want to haul her right off to bed. His. But he had played right along knowing that as soon as she figured the coast was clear, she wouldn't waste time coming here, to this lab where she assumed Dr. Chambers was hard at work during the night.

Over dinner he had been fully aware she'd been pumping him for information. And when she thought she had accumulated enough to make an appearance in the lab, she had begun feigning total exhaustion.

It was time to switch gears with Ainsley since the woman was too willful for her own good. They had played this game long enough. He wanted her and whether she admitted it or not, she wanted him.

Winston felt that he was very astute when it came to women and although she said one thing, he was very much aware her body was saying another and tonight he intended to prove it to her. After all, nobody told her to go snooping around in his house at this hour of the night. She had come in search of Dr. Chambers and he was going to make sure that's what she got. His gaze swept the laboratory where he spent most of his time. The space wasn't exactly conducive for seduction, but a man had to do what a man had to do. At least there was that cot on the other side of the room, the one he used occasionally to take power naps.

Placing down his wine glass, he picked up the remote that controlled the lightning in the room. Immediately the room was thrown into darkness, except for the brightness from the computer screen. When she opened the lab's door, she wouldn't see him at first. But she would eventually. And then it would be on.

Reaching what Ainsley figured had to be the laboratory, she leaned close and pressed her ear to the door. She didn't hear a sound. What if this was the one night Dr. Chambers had decided not to work late and retired to bed already? If that was the case, she would certainly be in a fix.

She drew in a deep breath thinking her wandering around in search of the doctor was madness and gave credence to just how desperate she was. Honestly, did she want her old job back that badly? She knew the answer to that one. It wasn't that she wanted her job as much as she needed a life outside of Claxton. If she didn't return to New York, then it would be someplace else because she doubted she would ever live again in her hometown.

Her parents were super and had been understanding. They'd also given her the support she needed. However, like most parents, they longed for the day she would settle down and give them a grandchild. Since she was their one and only, that meant the task fell solely on her.

Then there was the thought of starting over at another paper, working her way back up to the top. That was something she'd rather not do, and to ensure that she didn't, all she needed was this story on Dr. Chambers.

Breathing in deeply, she reached up and knocked softly on the door. When she didn't get a response, she held her breath and knocked again. She let out a sigh of relief when she heard a somewhat muffled voice say, "Come in."

Knowing this was probably her one and only shot, she drew in another deep breath, opened the door and quickly stepped inside, firmly closing it shut behind her. The last thing she needed was for Winston to show up and ruin everything by snatching away her golden opportunity.

She adjusted her eyes to the lack of light and glanced around. Surely the man wouldn't be working in the dark. "Dr. Chambers," she called out softly, not wanting to admit that being here was beginning to give her the creeps. Maybe she should have thought things through more before deciding to track down the man.

Suddenly, the air surrounding her stilled and the next thing she knew she was shoved back against the door. She opened her mouth to scream when a husky voice asked, "What are you doing here?"

Ainsley closed her mouth upon recognizing that voice

and noticed how his hands had closed around her waist, holding her firmly against the door. She tried to ignore the prickling of awareness his touch elicited. "Why is it that you're always manhandling me?" she snapped.

"Maybe you should ask yourself why it is that you always put yourself in a position to be manhandled. Twice you've come to this island uninvited and now you're someplace where you don't belong. That only leads me to believe one thing."

Although she had a feeling he couldn't see it, she slanted him a hostile look. "And what one thing is that?"

"That you like my hands on you. Rough or easy."

His words pissed her off and abruptly she lifted her chin. "I don't want your hands on me. I didn't know you were here. I assumed I was meeting with Dr. Chambers."

She saw the whiteness of his teeth when he smiled. "So you deliberately disobeyed me."

Yes, she had and maybe she should feel some remorse for doing so, especially since he'd given her shelter for the night, but she didn't. All she could think about was that he'd blown her one and only chance for that interview which had her seeing red. She stiffened her spine and squared her shoulders. "And what if I did?"

"Then I'm going to make sure you pay." And then he leaned in and took possession of her mouth.

The moment his tongue entered Ainsley's mouth every single remnant of Winston's control took a flying leap. Her taste combined with her scent was so overwhelming that he couldn't help but gather her closer, hold her tighter and kiss her more deeply.

She'd hesitated only for a quick second before kissing him back with just as much passion. That led him to believe he'd been right. She liked his hands on her and she'd been on the edge of losing control just like he had.

Whether she ever admitted it or not, that first night had impacted them both. He had finally accepted it. Although he could understand the why of it, there was more to it than just the scent of her and how her aroma had remained in his nostrils or the way she felt in his arms or tasted on his tongue. There was a primitive male need to bed her again, as if she was his mate for—

He tore his mouth from hers when he saw the crazy path his thoughts had begun to travel. He didn't need to be fooled by any notion that this or any woman was meant for him. There was no reason to think she was different than Caroline.

Breathing deeply, he stared down at her, looked into her eyes and felt all kinds of emotions while doing so. He couldn't remember ever being so sexually aware of a woman. At that moment he was filled with an urge to strip her naked, touch her and taste her all over, make love to her while attempting to find that deep connection they'd shared the last time, a connection so profound his insides were smoldering. The one he couldn't forget or shake off, no matter how hard he tried.

She was as stubborn as he was and had proven that, like him, she went after whatever she wanted and refused to let anything stand in her way. They would continue to be at an impasse unless new guidelines were established since the old ones weren't working.

"My ultimatum that you have to sleep with me to get an interview with Dr. Chambers is off the table," he leaned in to say against her moist lips. "You'll get the interview with him tomorrow regardless. I give you my word."

Her pulse quickened. Had he just said she would get the interview with Dr. Chambers? And that the proposition he'd made and that she hadn't agreed to was off the table? "What's the catch, Winston?"

He nibbled the corners of her mouth. "No catch," he said in a low husky voice, lifting the hem of her blouse and sliding his hand over her skin, driven with a need to touch her.

"And no more deals," he added. With a flick of his wrist, he undid the front clasp to her bra and within seconds her breasts were freed. He cupped them in his hands, caressed the tight buds of her nipples with his fingertips and heard her moan his name. "Like I said, regardless of whether you sleep with me tonight or not, you'll get the interview."

She drew in a deep breath, struggling to keep a level head, fully aware he was trying to seduce her and succeeding. "Can you make that kind of decision for Dr. Chambers?"

"Yes, I can and I will."

She lifted a brow. "Why?"

The corners of his mouth curved. "Because I'm hoping you enjoyed what we shared the last time and that you want to repeat it, for no other reason than because we want each other. No coercion on either of our parts. No game playing and no deals. Just total and complete satisfaction."

She hadn't expected this. *No game playing and no deals. Just total and complete satisfaction.* If she was honest with herself, she would admit there was something about their night together that she couldn't let go of. Something that had made her regret running out the next morning and had left her wondering how things would have been had she stayed.

"I want you so much I ache," he said in a voice that sounded surprisingly tender. He stepped closer and she could feel his hard erection throbbing against her stomach. "Are you willing to admit this desire between us is a mutual thing? And that you want me as much as I want you?" The velvety huskiness of his voice was intimate against her ear. His hot breath set off an erotic throbbing at the juncture of her thighs.

He lifted his head and she stared at him for what seemed like a long moment, feeling the need for him seep into her pores and drench her insides. She was painfully aware he was staring back at her, daring her to deny the intense desire that flowed between them.

Finally, when she couldn't take any more of his mental seduction, she leaned close to him and whispered, "Yes, I'm willing to admit it. I want you."

Chapter 11

That was all Winston needed to hear and quickly scooped up Ainsley into his arms. He thought about carrying her to his bedroom on the other side of the house but knew he didn't have the fortitude to make it that far.

He immediately crossed the room to the cot and placed her on it, grateful it was large and sturdy enough to hold their combined weight. He began tearing out of his clothes and watched as she didn't waste time getting out of hers. He leaned down to remove his shoes.

"Winston?"

He looked up at her, saw she was no longer getting undressed and suddenly a dreadful thought seeped into his mind that she had changed her mind. He drew in a deep, ragged breath when he was unable to read her thoughts. He swallowed the deep lump in his throat. "Yes?"

"I want you to take off my clothes. I like it when you do it."

He straightened to his full height. The relief he felt was so intense every muscle in his body began shivering. "I'd be glad to do so, sweetheart."

Sweetheart?

Where the hell had that come from? Terms of endearment were something he didn't toss out lightly. To be honest he didn't use them at all, not since Caroline. He used them all the time with her and she hadn't deserved a single one.

Erasing thoughts of Caroline from his mind, he kicked aside his shoes and strolled naked over to Ainsley. He didn't speak, just maintained a visual contact that was so intense he could feel it in every part of his body. He wondered what she was thinking when she lifted her hips so he could tug the jeans down her legs. What consumed her mind as she stared deeply into his eyes with the same single-minded focus as he was staring into hers? He wondered if at any point in time he'd felt this much need for a woman, this much desire and knew that he hadn't.

When he had her undressed to just her panties, he stopped before removing her final piece of clothing and he continued to hold her gaze. The small smile that curved her lips was a total turn-on and he hadn't known such a gesture could make him want her even more.

He had to make love to her and he had to do it now. Hard. Raw. They would deal with finesse the next time. But at that moment he had to get inside her. Take her with the intensity he felt in every part of his body.

He quivered when his fingers brushed her skin as he eased her panties down her legs. The electrical charge between them was so strong the air nearly sizzled. For one quick moment he had a feeling of possessiveness and his heart missed several beats at the absurdity of such a thought.

Winston took a step back when she was completely naked and let his gaze roam all over her. His mind kept reiterating, if you've seen one female body, then you've seen them all. But he knew that was a lie, especially when it came to Ainsley St. James. She was in a class all by herself.

Then there was the passion the two of them could stir. Always hot and steamy when they were of one accord and not on opposing sides. They both wanted this. No egos involved. No deals to be made any longer. The thought that he would be getting another night with her sent sensations rushing through him that were almost overwhelming.

For a while there was silence between them as their gazes fused. Then he broke the contact to reach for his jeans and retrieve a condom out of the pocket. He was about to sheath himself when he glanced over at her and caught her watching him and it stirred something deep within him, made his groin tighten. He eased toward her, placed his knee on the cot and reached out to her and she took his hand and came to him willingly. He couldn't let himself think just how much this moment meant to him, how he had dreamed about it happening again. How much he had wanted it.

Taken away by those thoughts, he wasn't aware of what Ainsley was about to do until he felt the wet tip of her tongue slide across his chest. He was one who believed in foreplay but wasn't sure he had the control for it tonight. And when the path of her tongue went lower, toward his stomach, his entire groin clenched.

"Ainsley..." He heard the sound of his own voice, a low growl of warning. He was too close to the edge and what she was doing could push him right over.

She lifted her head and her gaze blazed into his. There was a hot and needy look in her eyes and at that moment he saw she was as close to the edge as he was. "I'd like to see you try and stop me," she warned back.

He couldn't help the way his lips curved into a smile. This woman was different than any woman he'd ever met.

She defied him at every turn, rarely saw eye to eye with him, refused to let him have his way and could hold her own against him and with him.

"Then do whatever you want," he murmured in a raw voice. The scent of her was doing a number on him, stroking his senses at the same time it was blinding his mind with heat and more heat. Intense. Torrid. Explosive.

And when she dipped her mouth lower he knew he was about to lose it.

Ainsley had known she was in danger of losing control the moment Winston had brought her over to the cot. She throbbed, all the way to her womb. How could she want a man so much? Even more so than she had that first night. There was nothing about him she didn't like…especially this, she thought as she came nearer his hard erection. What was there about it that made it like a magnet to her mouth, solace to her tongue? What was this desperation in her to taste him again?

She eased him into her mouth and could actually hear herself groan in pleasure at the same time she noted how Winston's breath rushed in through his teeth. That was all she recalled before her mouth went to work on him. She became lost in her own world. He seemed to grow bigger in her mouth and it seemed she made whatever adjustment was necessary to accommodate him.

"Can't take any more," he moaned just seconds before he pulled out of her mouth and he tumbled her backward on the cot. Lifting her legs to his shoulders, he slid himself over her body and between her widened legs. At that moment she was all too conscious of him, too fully aware of all the sensations she was feeling and the need that was bubbling inside her. Her blood was roaring through her veins.

And when he held tight to her hips and slid inside her,

she cried out in blissful pleasure. And when he pressed even farther inside of her and began stroking her, moving in and out of her with slow yet thorough thrusts, she heard herself practically beg. "Winston...please."

He knew what she was asking for and quickened the pace, set the rhythm, pounding into her, driving deep into her. Then she felt the heat of his mouth on her skin, laving her while stroking her inside. Her response was wild as she lifted her hips off the cot, arching upward to meet him stroke for stroke.

Then he leaned down and kissed her, took possession of her mouth as if he had every right to do so. And she knew at that moment they were both completely out of control. The more he pumped himself into her, the more she arched her body to take him deeper.

Then something within her snapped and she screamed as her body was thrown into intense spasms. She heard him scream her name as well and his hold on her tightened as he began pounding into her with the speed of a jackhammer.

Another orgasm ripped through her and she felt her body fragment into a thousand pieces. Her heart skipped several beats with the greed of his kiss and she returned them with a level of desire she couldn't contain. Waves of ecstasy consumed her and the last thing she remembered was him pulling back from the kiss and whispering in a low, intimate growl, "You're incredible." And then adding with a throaty huskiness, "I want you again."

Hours later Winston opened his eyes. The first thing he noted was a sleeping Ainsley stretched on top of him, her head coming to a rest beneath his jaw. The second thing he noticed through the high windows was that dawn had broken and the sun was out. The storm had passed.

He closed his eyes as remnants of last night flashed

through his mind. The way he had taken Ainsley on this cot, the number of times he'd done so. But the way he saw it, she'd taken him as well, without shame, without concern for finesse, but with a fierce need that had matched his own. Some sort of primitive indulgence and frantic excitement had enflamed their hunger for each other, compelled them to seek out and capture that level of incredible pleasure they could only experience with each other.

He had driven her wild with passion and she had pushed him beyond the confines of any restraints. Never had he thrust so hard and deep within a woman. Never had a woman screamed his name the way she had, or arched her body like a bowstring to meet his repeated strokes.

He didn't want to think about how many condoms he'd gone through last night and was glad he'd had a half dozen or so stuffed in a small box under the cot. This was the first time he'd ever made love to a woman in here, but he'd prepared himself for Ainsley. After all, he believed in operating on the cautious side when handling his business. And last night he had definitely handled his business while allowing her a chance to handle hers. Their desire was mutual, their lust incredibly erotic, and in the end their satisfaction was off the charts.

Now with a new day came promises that had to be kept. And as he watched her sleep peacefully atop him, he knew he would keep them and wondered how she would handle finding out he was Chambers. Would she care as long as she got a story? Yes, she would care and might even go so far as to think she'd been taken advantage of. That meant he had to do whatever was needed to make sure she didn't feel that way. And why did he care exactly? Hell, he wasn't sure, but he did.

She shifted a little and his erection began throbbing and he knew the exact moment it reached its full potential and poked her in the stomach. Her eyes flickered opened and immediately connected with his. Her smile stretched across her beautiful lips. "Good morning."

"Good morning." He then pulled on one of her spiral curls and brought her mouth down to his. Moments later when he finally released her mouth, he breathed softly against her moist lips and said, "You're beautiful in the morning."

Her heart was racing; he could feel it where her chest was plastered to his. "Last night was wonderful," he said, wanting to get it out there. There was no way he couldn't when every fiber of his being felt revitalized.

"It was incredible," she countered, leaning closer and placing soft kisses at the corner of his lips.

He smiled. "That, too. I suppose we should get up."

"I suppose we should."

But then he felt it in the air—that charge of excitement, sexual desire, need and greed. "Maybe later."

His hands gripped her hips, lifted her…and then he remembered. He'd used all the condoms. All the others were in his bedroom. "We have a problem. No more condoms in here."

She met his gaze. "No problem. I'm on birth control and I'm in good health. What about you?"

"No problem with me."

"Good."

She straddled his erection already standing straight up for her entry and he moaned deep in his throat when she eased down on it, stretching her wide as he entered her.

A smile of unadulterated satisfaction curved his lips when he had maxed to the hilt inside of her. His shaft throbbed even more at the feel of being skin to skin with her. And then she began moving, riding him like she had the night before and he knew at that moment as rapid sensations tore through him that this was a ride he would remember for a long time.

Chapter 12

"So...when do I get to meet Dr. Chambers?

Winston met Ainsley's gaze and knew the moment for reckoning had arrived. He breathed in a deep sigh, wondering what would be the best way to tell her the truth and make sure she understood why he hadn't come clean before now.

After making love that morning, they had gotten out of bed and showered together. There had been something extra exciting and thrilling about taking her against that shower wall, then lathering her body, then taking the hand-held sprayer and rinsing her off before taking her all over again and kissing her hungrily while a stream of water rained down on them.

They had tossed her clothes in the laundry again while she put on a bathrobe. By the time her clothes had washed and dried, they had eaten the brunch he had prepared.

Now she was fully dressed and they were feeding Lucy and Ricky. It was close to noon already which was probably the reason Ainsley had begun getting antsy. The meeting couldn't get put off any longer.

"Come on, let's go for a walk on the beach and look for your duffel bag. Dr. Chambers will be ready for introductions when we get back."

He saw the way his words brought an automatic smile to her face. "Thanks. Finally. But I can't help being a little nervous about it."

Winston used the hose to wash out the pails that had contained the dolphins' food. He glanced over at her. "Why? He's just a man."

She was sitting on one of the stools he kept in the area to use when he conducted his daily lessons with Ricky and Lucy. "Yes, but he's a renowned scientist of marine life. I did my research and so far he hasn't granted an interview to anyone. Being his bodyguard I'm sure you know that."

Winston was silent for a minute and then he said, "Then you need to think about what it means for him to be granting one to you."

"Trust me, I do. But I know you had something to do with it. You can't convince me he would be seeing me if you hadn't put in a good word for me at some point. You don't know what getting this interview means to me."

He put aside the hose and reached his hand out to her. "Then tell me...during our walk."

Leaving the house, they followed the oyster-shell path to the wooden steps that led down to the beach. The day after the hard storm had brought in wind and a little chill. The sun was no longer bright in the sky but was now hiding behind a row of clouds and the ocean waves were beating fast and furious against the shoreline.

In the distance she heard the powerful sound of boat engines, which meant the owners were eager to be back on the water again, even with the brisk wind and choppy waves.

Winston had loaned her one of his jackets and she tightened it around her as they began walking, making shoe prints in the sand. For a while neither of them said anything. His hands were in his pockets and a part of her missed seeing them—strong hands that could make her tremble from a single touch. Hands that could incite a need within her when they caressed her in certain places.

Ainsley drew in the poignant scent of the ocean but even that couldn't erode the scent of the man walking beside her. Directly after their shower he had smelled like soap; now he simply smelled like Winston.

"So, why is it so important for you to interview Dr. Chambers, Ainsley?"

She glanced over at him. In all honesty, she had very little to lose by telling him the truth. He'd given his word and she believed him. Besides, maybe he would understand why she'd been so persistent. "I had a nice job with *The New York Times,* had worked my way up to staff reporter with a weekly column. I interviewed people making news and use the name A. Saint James on my byline. With the column came a plush office, administrative assistant and recognition…. It was a nice setup, one I felt was well-deserved. I'd worked my tail off to get it."

She paused for a moment, remembering the hard work, the long hours and dedication to make a mark at such a young age. She probably would still have been climbing that ladder if she hadn't broken that story on Senator Morris. No one would have known the staunch conservative had more than a few skeletons in his closet. And that someone who'd known about those skeletons was putting the squeeze to get him to vote against certain legislation. She wasn't sure why she had been the one to get the anonymous tip, but she had.

"And?"

Winston's question made her realize her thoughts had digressed. "And I gave it all up because I thought my hometown needed me. I returned to Claxton, New Jersey, to run for mayor."

She paused a moment, remembering how hard it had been to make that decision and how she believed she would have the backing of the majority of the town.

"I thought it was going to be a pretty easy win for me. After all, I was a hometown girl and my opponent hadn't lived in Claxton for more than a year, so I felt I was the town's favorite. Their favorite daughter, so to speak, especially since one of my ancestors founded the town close to a hundred years ago."

She paused again before saying, "I hadn't expected a nasty campaign. My opponent made up a lot of lies, smeared my good name, and what hurt more than anything was that people who'd known me all my life actually believed them."

Ainsley leaned down to pick up a seashell and thought it was beautiful. A keepsake. "I lost and intended to go back to New York, but my father had a heart attack the day after the election. I'm convinced all that nastiness during the campaign took a toll on him. I'm the only child and my father and I were close. It hurt him to see the townspeople turn on me that way."

She drew in a deep breath. "I remained in Claxton to help Mom out with Dad, who'd never been sick a day in his life. I was so busy helping my parents that I kind of forgot about the election until it was time for the inauguration. I decided with Dad doing better that this would be the perfect time to get away since Claxton was the last place I wanted to be during that week."

"What happens when you go back?"

"I'll be there long enough to pack up my stuff and move

back to New York. Luckily I subleased my place and the couple will be out by the end of the month, so things are falling nicely into place for me. But my job isn't a sure thing yet. My boss might be able to rehire me if I can get the interview with Dr. Chambers. Bobby received a tip that the doctor is working on something big. Plus Bobby wants dibs on that new sexual enhancement drug before the FDA."

Winston didn't say anything. He could have interrupted and told her that thanks to Charley, he knew the story of her short political career and her father's illness. But listening to her tell it had put a whole new perspective on things, filled in some blanks.

"I have to admit that getting my old job back might have been the factor driving me initially, however..."

He glanced over at her. "However, what?"

"Now I'm intrigued. Why would someone so accomplished want to be a recluse and not toot their own horn? Why not give interviews and let the world know who he is and what he's about?"

"He has his reasons," Winston said quietly.

"And you know what they are?"

Winston stopped walking and scanned the ocean waters. The shrimpers joined the boaters, with sea gulls swarming in their wake. In the distance he could see the nets being tossed in the water, anticipating a good catch. At one time his grandfather had owned a shrimp boat that had plied up and down the Port Royal Sound. Captain Jeremy Coltrane was well known in these parts and loved Barrett Shores. Winston loved this place as well, always had and always would. It was in his blood the same way it had been with his ancestors before him.

He glanced back at Ainsley, deciding to respond to her question as to whether he knew the reason Chambers didn't grant interviews. "Yes, I know his reasons, and if he wants you to know, he will tell you. Come on, it's time to go back."

"And meet Dr. Chambers?" she asked in a hopeful voice.

He held her gaze for a moment before reaching out his hand to take hers in his. "Yes, and meet Dr. Chambers."

A chilling dread washed over Winston as he sat across the room and watched Ainsley as she nervously paced. When they had returned from the beach, he'd assumed admitting the truth would be easy but he found it wasn't. A part of him figured although she would be upset, she wouldn't turn her back on the chance to do the interview. Yet another part of him knew that regardless, he needed her to understand why he'd put off telling her until now.

"While we're waiting, I think I need to clear up a few things," he decided to say.

She stopped pacing and turned to him. "What?"

"Barrett Shores belongs to the Coltrane family."

He saw the surprise that lit her eyes as she perched her hip on the arm of the sofa. "But I thought that—"

"Yes, I know what you thought," he interrupted her. "So I figured I needed to clear that up now."

He watched as she slid her curvy frame off the arm of the sofa and into the seat. "How did your family come to own an island?" she asked. "I assume it's being leased to Dr. Chambers to use as a marine sanctuary for his work."

"I had a hunch that's what you figured," he said, getting up from his chair to cross the room to the wine decanter. He turned toward her. "Would you like a glass?"

"Yes, please."

He poured two glasses of wine and strolled over to hand her one. He had decided to open a few of the windows and the breeze blowing through caused the curtains to stir. The scent of the ocean mingled with that of yellow jasmines that were growing practically everywhere on the island.

He reclaimed his chair in time to watch her take a sip of wine and thought the way her mouth fit the glass was one of the most erotic things he'd ever seen. He could feel his gut stirring and tried pushing the feeling aside knowing he needed to focus on their discussion.

"Have you ever heard of Robert Small?"

She scrunched up her brow for a second. "No, I don't recall the name."

He nodded. "Small was well-known in these parts many years ago. He was a slave who, along with my great-great-great-great-grandfather Isaac Coltrane, made a daring escape during the Civil War."

She sipped her wine. "How?"

"By commandeering a Confederate ship, *CSS Planter,* and turning it over to Union officers."

He could tell by the light in her eyes that what he'd said had interested her. "Really?" she said, leaning in to hear what else he had to say.

"Yes. Robert grew up on a plantation in Beaufort. Isaac was born here. At the time it was called Barrett Plantation. The two slaves met as kids. The masters of both plantations were brothers and it wasn't uncommon to bring some of their slaves along whenever they visited each other."

She nodded and took another sip of her wine. "How did they learn to navigate a ship?"

"Small's master was a captain and took him on several voyages with him. Both Small and Isaac worked the docks in Charleston and became very knowledgeable of the Charleston waterways."

Winston took a sip of his own wine and continued. "Small and Isaac came up with this plan. If they were successful, it meant freedom. If they failed, it meant death. They were willing to take their chances."

"How did they carry it out?"

Winston wanted to keep talking and keep her interested, so he could ease his way into what she needed to know. "The captain of the *Planter* decided to dock for a little R & R, took his crew with him and left behind his eight slaves. Foolish of the captain to think, since they were uneducated, they also didn't have a lick of sense."

He paused a moment and then said, "With Small taking over as captain and Isaac as his first mate, they decided to use the ship and make a run for it."

A half smile touched her lips. "I'm happy for them but sad they had to leave their families behind."

Winston chuckled. "Says who?"

Ainsley's eyes widened. "They had hidden their families on board as stowaways?"

"No. They'd instructed their kin to be on a nearby wharf hiding out. The ship made its first stop there and collected everybody. And by everybody, I mean Small's family and the families of his crew members."

Her smile widened. "That included Isaac's wife?"

He shook his head. "No, he was single and his parents had died years earlier. His only sister, Ruth, had been sold away to another plantation in Georgia when she was ten."

"Oh. That's sad."

"Then let's get back to talking about happy stuff," he said, taking another sip of wine. "With everyone of importance on board, they made their daring escape by heading for Union waters. And what I forgot to tell you was that one of the things they had on board—that had been left behind by the good captain—was the all-important Confederate code book that contained a lot of information that would be detrimental if it fell into the Union's hands."

He watched how she shifted positions on the sofa and tucked her legs beneath her. She had gotten so pulled into the story that for the time being she had forgotten about the fact she was waiting for Dr. Chambers to make an appearance.

"So what information was in this all-important code book?" she asked.

He stretched out his legs in front of him. He hadn't told the story of his family's history in a long time and didn't recall telling another woman…since Caroline. "Important info such as special Confederate secret signals, the location of mines in and around the Charleston Harbor and planned water attacks of the Union fleet."

"You're kidding!"

"I kid you not. Small, Isaac and the crew succeeded, steering the ship right into Union waters. They were awarded for their bravery by President Lincoln. Pulling off such a feat proved to be invaluable to the Union army. At the end of the Civil War, Small became the owner of his former master's home and over fifteen hundred acres of land. He later went into politics and was elected to the South Carolina House of Representatives."

"And Isaac?" she inquired.

"He became the owner of this island and came here to live, changed the name to Barrett Shores. But first he went looking for and found his baby sister. And he met and fell in love with the woman who happened to be his sister's best friend. A young woman by the name of Judith. He brought them both to live here. He married Judith a few months later."

Ainsley didn't say anything and then wiped at her eyes. "That was an incredible and beautiful story, Winston. And your family has been living here since?"

"Yes, but there were challenges. Hurricanes, floods

and developers determined to get this island at any and all costs."

"But your family survived and held on."

It was a statement and not a question so he responded as such. "Yes, they survived and held on. Six generations of Coltranes have lived on Barrett Shores…including R. J. Chambers."

She lifted a brow. "Are you saying that you and Dr. Chambers are related?"

"Actually, Ainsley, it's closer than that."

She frowned in confusion. "Is he your grandfather?"

At the shake of his head, she then asked, "Your father? Uncle?"

When he didn't claim any of those, she threw her hands up in frustration. "What then?"

Winston didn't say anything. Instead for one long tense moment he sat there and stared at her and she stared back. Waiting. Then he got up and slowly walked across the room to stand in front of her. He could see the anxious expression on her face.

He knew the best thing to do was to come out with it, so he did. "Dr. R. J. Chambers is a pseudonym."

Surprise lit her eyes. "For whom?"

Leaning in and bracing his arms on either sides of her, Winston bent down until they were nearly nose to nose. "For me."

Chapter 13

Ainsley's jaw dropped and she stared at him as her anger began rising. His words were like a blow delivered not only to her senses but to every part of her body. And she simply stared at him while the truth of his words filtered through her mind, her sight and her good old common sense. Had she taken the time to use them, she would have figured this out herself. Wouldn't she? She rubbed the back of her neck, not so sure.

"Why? Why didn't you tell me the truth from the beginning?" she asked, feeling as if steam was about to come out of her ears.

He leaned back in a cocky stance and crossed his arms over his chest. "And why should I have?"

Now that did it. She eased up from her chair and, poking his chest as if to punctuate her words, she said loud enough to wake the dead, "Because you were trying to swap sex for the interview!"

"No, if you recall, I'd already had you. What I proposed, as a way of a swap, was for you to do what you'd said you'd do anyway so that I could get some more of you. But I tossed that idea out the window when I decided to give you the interview regardless of whether we made love again or not."

His words only served as a sharp reminder of how she was taken in by him. "You led me to believe Dr. Chambers existed."

"And he does exist to anyone who doesn't know me, Ainsley," he said, dropping his hands from across his chest to put them into his pockets. "On the beach you asked me why someone so accomplished would want to be a recluse and not toot their own horn. I'll tell you the reason I've worked under an alias for the last seven years. So I wouldn't be hounded by reporters. So why would I drop my guise for you? A reporter who only wanted an interview? I didn't know you and I damn sure didn't trust you."

"But you had slept with me!" she snapped.

He cocked his head to the side. "And?"

At that moment she couldn't answer because he was reminding her that whatever they had shared had been nothing more than sex. "And nothing, I guess. I'm not a fool. You had condoms ready under your pillow that night, which meant you had planned to sleep with a woman. Do you deny it?"

"No."

His honesty wasn't supposed to bother her but it did. "So, it was all about sex."

"Of course it was all about sex…at least that night it was. And because it was all about sex, I didn't need to know your occupation. It wouldn't have mattered to me if you'd been a teacher, reporter, pilot or whatever."

He paused a moment and then added, "It didn't matter because I wanted you. And when you showed up again as a reporter, it should have mattered but in a way it didn't because I still wanted you. And I discovered, although your defiance was wearing on my last nerve, that's the one thing I admire most about you. You don't know the meaning of giving up."

She placed her hands on her hips. "If that's supposed to be a compliment, I don't want it."

He shrugged. "But you're going to take it whether you want it or not, Ainsley St. James. Because you and I both know you're not a quitter, no matter what. Even when Luis Higgins tried to shame you into dropping out of that mayoral race, you wouldn't."

Shock contorted her face. "Y-y-you knew about that… even before I—I told you?" she stammered in anger.

"Yes. I had Charley do a background check on you after your first visit."

She'd heard enough. "I'm leaving!" she said, moving around him.

"No, you're not. Like I said, you're not a quitter. Besides, you've told me what this interview means to you," he said to her retreating back.

She turned around. "You can take the interview and shove it up your—"

"I wouldn't make that suggestion if I were you," he said, standing with his feet braced apart and his hands deep in his pockets. "Think about it, Ainsley. No matter how mad you are with me right now, when you see things logically, you'll realize you're the winner in this, not me. I'm breaking one of my strictest rules for you. I am granting you and only you an exclusive interview. Because I like you and you have spunk. And I believe in your integrity. I believe you will do the right thing with the interview, so I'm willing to take a chance and open myself up to you."

She stared at him a long moment and then asked, "Why?"

He held her gaze. "When someone believes in you, there's no need for further doubt. And I believe in you."

His words gave her pause and she drew in a deep breath and tried to think rationally. *He believed in her.* At that moment she realized just what a risk he was taking in doing that because she *was* a reporter. And she knew more than anyone that some reporters would do or say just about anything for a story. There was a reason he used an alias in lieu of receiving credit for his work as Winston Coltrane. Why was he hiding behind the illusion of Dr. R. J. Chambers, an old recluse? He was willing to let her invade his private world to find those answers.

"Okay. I'm going to do the interview but we need to get a few things straight right now," she said, stiffening her spine and narrowing her gaze on him. In spite of herself she felt her heart fluttering at the way he was standing there, in that sexy position, with his eyes boring into hers in an unnerving way.

She released an agitated sigh when she came to a stop in front of him. "From here on out things are strictly professional between us. And if you think for one minute I'll have sex with you again…ever…then you have another thought coming."

He smiled and she tried to ignore the way her breath caught in her throat. When he didn't say anything, just stood there with that damn gorgeous smile on his face, she decided she needed space from him. "I'm getting my things out of the dryer and going to the guest room for a while," she said backing up.

"Okay."

To her way of thinking, he sounded too agreeable. She quickly headed toward the laundry room.

"Ainsley…" he murmured in that oh-too-throaty voice. Something told her to keep walking and ignore him but for some reason she couldn't. She turned back to him. "What?" she all but snapped.

He gave her that damn smile again. "A few moments ago, you said if I think for one minute that we'll have sex again…ever…then I have another thought coming."

She lifted her chin. "And?"

"Figured I'd let you know, it's coming."

She frowned and lifted her brow. "What's coming?"

"Another thought."

Winston was very much aware the woman was pretty pissed with him, but he couldn't help it. It was either goad her or cross the room and kiss her, and heaven help him, he wanted to kiss her but doubted he could stop with just a kiss. He would want to strip her naked and—

"This is all a joke to you, isn't it?"

"No. There's nothing comical about what I want to do to you, Ainsley," he said smoothly. "Want to hear them?"

"I suggest you keep your thoughts to yourself." She then turned and walked out of the room.

Winston watched her leave thinking the woman was simply incredible, and she was getting under his skin the way he knew he was getting under hers. Like he told her, the interview would be interesting. Mainly because he had no intentions of keeping his hands to himself. She would learn that when you played with fire you were liable to get burned.

Works both ways, bro.

Winston went completely still, not liking that particular thought. He had gotten burned once and would never let it happen again. Some men could get over hurt and betrayal; unfortunately he wasn't one of them. He was a bachelor not taken, not spoken for. Free. Available.

A bachelor unclaimed.

And come hell or high water, he intended to stay that way.

The sound of his cell phone cut through his thoughts and he pulled the phone out of his back pocket upon recognizing the ring tone. It was Virgil. Perfect timing. If there was any person that could remind him of the importance of staying free of the female population—except when it became physically necessary—it was Virgil. Like Winston, Virgil had fallen in love young and had learned a hard lesson.

Virgil's woman hadn't betrayed him but she'd done something almost as bad. She had accused him of betraying her, a lie fed by her sister. Virgil hadn't taken the false accusations lightly.

"V? What's up?" Winston asked.

"Nothing much. Just checking on the mad scientist. Heard you'd come off the island for a spell."

He didn't have to wonder where Virgil had heard that. News always got around among the godbrothers. "Yes, but I'm back at work now. Have you talked to the others lately?" he asked, knowing he'd been lax in touching base with them. He hadn't talked to them in a week or so.

"Yes, everyone is alive and breathing. Looking forward to all of us getting together at York's anniversary party in New York. Z plans to attend, as well."

Winston was glad to hear that. Zion, a world renowned jewelry maker, was living in Rome.

They conversed a little while longer and just talking to his godbrother helped put things in prospective. Virgil, with all his bitterness, animosity and don't-give-a-damn attitude, had a way of doing that.

A few moments later their conversation ended and Winston knew he had to leave for a while and do something he enjoyed, something that could ease his mind of all these crazy thoughts where Ainsley was concerned.

He headed up the stairs to his bedroom to grab his jacket.

* * *

Ainsley repacked her duffel bag. Earlier that day they had located the bag, but not where it had been left. The heavy rains had floated it twenty feet away. All the items inside had gotten soiled and had needed to be washed. She'd just folded the last piece of clothing when she heard the door slam shut. Evidently Winston had left. Good riddance. But then of course he would be back at some point since he lived here.

She figured the interview couldn't be done in a single afternoon, not even a single day. She wanted to know everything there was about Winston Coltrane, aka Dr. R. J. Chambers.

She suddenly recalled what he'd said about how he'd researched information about her, and deciding not to be outdone, she quickly made her way to the kitchen where the huge panel board was lit up.

"Charley," she said with authority. "I want information on Winston Coltrane."

"Affirmative. Information destination?"

Information destination? Making a wild guess at what he was asking, she gave him her email address and her smile widened when he said, *"Information sent. Delivery time one minute."*

She didn't have her laptop with her, but she did have her iPhone and could read the information from there. Winston would find out in good time that not only was she not a quitter, she was a woman who didn't take being made a fool of very well, either.

Glancing out the window at the sound of a boat's motor, she watched as Winston steered a nice-looking vessel from the dock. She couldn't wait to interview him and if he thought she would make things easy for him, then he was dead wrong.

She continued to watch until his boat looked like a speck out there in the middle of the ocean. Had he gone to cool off? Heck, what was he mad about? She was the one who'd been the joke of the day. But she intended to do what her grandmother always told her.

When someone gives you lemons, make lemonade.

Winston paused when his foot touched the top plank of the deck to his house. Was that music?

He frowned. It wasn't just any music, it was that loud hip-hop stuff that he'd never gotten into. Probably because whenever he went to visit Evan out in L.A., he had to be subjected to it. His brother ate, breathed and practically slept with rap and was so entrenched in the hip-hop culture it was downright sickening. So why was it being played in his house?

He opened the door that led into the space between the kitchen and laundry room and stopped short. Ainsley was on the floor exercising. At least that's what he thought she was doing, lying flat on her back with her legs kicking up in the air. And she was wearing the same outfit she had used to climb the flagpole.

He silently closed the door behind him and continued to watch her and it soon became obvious she wasn't exercising but was doing part of a dance routine. He then remembered what he'd read in the report about her having been a dancer.

She had danced up a sweat and her skin was practically glistening. Wouldn't take much to tempt him to cross the room and begin licking it off. He then shook his head thinking what he was really tempted to do was to knock himself in the head. Already he had forgotten about the reason he had stayed away on his boat all afternoon.

He had needed the time to screw his head back on right where this particular woman was concerned. And now all it took was seeing her working her legs and ass to hip-hop music to cause his insides to turn to mush.

Breaking his stare, he moved away from the door and walked over to the boom box—*his* boom box—and turned it off. That got her attention and she turned in his direction. A part of him wished she hadn't done that when he couldn't help but clearly see her hard nipples through the leotard. Immediately his stomach began clenching.

"Hey," she called out to him, placing her hands on her hips. "What do you think you're doing?"

His eyes narrowed. "What do you think you're doing?" he countered.

"What does it look like? I'm dancing."

"Why?"

"Why what?" she asked.

"Why are you dancing?"

She shrugged. "Because I like to. No, I take that back, I *love* to dance. I like dancing better than anything."

He wondered if that included sex.

"It relaxes me," she added.

Like boating relaxed him, he mused. But nothing was better to him than sex, and sex with her was off the charts. "Well, I don't like the music."

"You don't like the music?" she repeated like she was certain she'd heard him wrong.

"Yes. I never married that hip-hop culture."

She grabbed a towel off one of the small tables and began wiping her face, her arms, different parts of her body. "So what kind of music do you listen to?" she asked and he drew his gaze away from her body and up to her face when she used the towel to wipe off sweat there.

"Anything other than hip-hop."

"Well, those CDs were in a closet in the bedroom you let me use. If they aren't yours, then whose are they?"

"Evan's."

She lifted a brow. "Who is Evan?"

"My brother."

"Evan Coltrane… Now where do I recall that name?" Her face then lit in an I-don't-believe-it expression. "Your brother is Evan Coltrane? The Evan Coltrane who used to play for the—"

"Yes," he said quickly. There was no need to let her go through the entire spiel. Evan's reputation as an outstanding player in the NFL preceded him. And before she slipped into her nosy-reporter mode and began asking questions about Evan, he said, "The interview can start tomorrow morning and hopefully you'll be through by noon," he said, heading into the kitchen.

"Don't count on it."

He stopped and turned toward her, certain he hadn't heard her right. "Excuse me?"

"I said don't count on the interview being over by noon tomorrow. In fact, I'm looking at it taking a good week at the most. Possibly two."

"What? Why would it take that much time to interview me?"

A smile curved her lips. "Because I see that you're a very complex man and I need time to delve deep into your persona."

Delve deep into his persona? Who did she think she was? Dr. Phil?

"In other words, Winston, I want to know what makes you happiest."

He leaned back against a wall, held her gaze, felt a deep throbbing in his gut. "Sex makes me happiest," he said bluntly.

She narrowed her gaze. "When it pertains to your work," she clarified.

He shrugged. "Sex still makes me happiest, which is why I study the mating habits of sea life and have come up with a way where it can benefit humans."

"Then I can't help but find your work interesting."

"Whatever," he said. "Come up with a list of questions and I'll highlight those I plan to answer."

"That's not the way I conduct an interview" was her brisk reply.

He couldn't help but smile at that. "Sorry, but that's the way you'll conduct mine."

Chapter 14

A few hours later, Ainsley glanced across the kitchen table at Winston. Once again he had prepared an outstanding meal, a pan of something he called low-country boil—that consisted of white potatoes, sausage, corn on the cob, crab meat and shrimp—all seasoned to taste, along with red rice, corn bread and collard greens.

She had offered to help but he'd turned her down again, saying he preferred working in his kitchen alone. So she had let him. Instead she had spent her time reading the information Charley had sent over her iPhone. It hadn't been a whole lot but what she'd read had been pretty interesting. His educational background was impressive and the fact that, at a young age, he had been a top marine biologist at the world's largest research-based pharmaceutical company. He had worked there for almost five years before resigning from a top-level position. She couldn't help wondering why, since he'd made a whole lot of money working there.

Another thing she found interesting, in fact rather fascinating, was that he had five godbrothers and was close to all of them. She had a godsister named Emily somewhere, but hadn't seen or talked to her in years. But from what she'd read, Winston and his godbrothers stayed in touch.

"You're quiet."

She waited until she was through chewing her food to reply. "You actually want to hear me talk?"

He shrugged. "I'm used to being here alone so the silence doesn't bother me. Usually I prefer it. But I have a feeling you're not used to not having anything to say so I'll make the sacrifice."

Ainsley took a sip of her wine cooler, which seemed most appropriate with their meal. "Are you trying to say in a roundabout way that I talk too much?"

He grinned. "No. In fact when you're not being nosy or persistent about something, I noticed you're a woman of few words."

Ainsley would have to agree with that. Some people were talkers and others observers. She did both when it suited her, preferably more observing. But since he brought it up...

"There are a few things I'd like to discuss with you," she said.

He held her gaze. "What things?"

"First of all, tell me about your five godbrothers."

His hand went still, holding his fork in midair. He didn't say anything for a minute. "How do you know about my godbrothers?"

She smiled sweetly. "You're not the only one who can get information from Charley."

For a moment he simply sat there and stared at her and then she saw the corners of his lips curve in a smile right before he laughed. "Like I said, you're persistent. Only thing, my godbrothers are off-limits and won't be included with the interview."

Waving off his words, she said, "This is not for the article. I'm asking for my own benefit."

He lifted a brow. "Why?"

That was a good question. How could she explain that she wanted to know as much about him as she could? She owed it to herself to do so. Okay, she had slept with him countless times when she hadn't known a lot about him, but there were a number of things she was curious about. "Let's just say I find them fascinating."

"You don't know them."

"Yes, but the whole idea of a person having five godbrothers is sort of overwhelming."

Winston didn't say anything for a moment while he sipped his wine cooler. Yes, he could see how it could be overwhelming to some people, but not to him. He and the five men had been born within twenty-four months of each other, with the exception of Zion who was the baby of the bunch. They had always been close and usually spent summers and holidays together while growing up.

So, okay, if she wanted to hear it, then he would tell her. He began talking, telling her how their fathers, the six best friends from Morehouse, had made a pledge on graduation day, a pledge they had each fulfilled. As expected she had asked her questions—lots of questions—and he thought she was going to topple over in her chair when he mentioned one of his godbrothers was Zion Blackstone, the world famous jewelry designer.

"Tell me more about your family," she said.

He took another sip of his wine cooler. "My parents moved away three years ago when my maternal grandparents became too much for my mom's sister to take care of by herself. They are living in Florida."

"How did your parents meet?" she asked.

"At college in Atlanta. Dad, as I mentioned, attended Morehouse and Mom was at Clark."

"What about your grandparents?"

He leaned forward over the table. "Maybe it was a mistake to start you to talking."

She chuckled and waved off his words. "Just answer the question, please."

He leaned back in his chair after noticing how her thick spiral curls actually fanned around her face. He didn't care for that particular style on some women, because a lot of them didn't have the shape of face to wear it. But the style looked good on her. The shape of her face was perfect.

"My grandfather and his father before him and all the other male Coltranes before them were shrimpers. It was a very lucrative business. Shrimps off the coast of Barrett Shores were the biggest and tastiest, and as a result were in high demand by restaurants along the east coast all the way up to Boston."

She nodded. "So what happened with the shrimp boat business?"

He took another sip of his wine cooler. "My grandfather felt it had run its course and wanted more for my father, who was his only son…and a very smart one at that. So he sent him to Morehouse and the shrimp boat business ended when my grandfather passed away around twenty years ago."

"So you knew your grandparents?"

"And my great-grandparents as well. Both lived to reach one hundred. Long lives are common in my family," he said.

"Who taught you how to cook?"

"My grandmother. She was a Gullah and passed her love for cooking down to me. I used to watch her when she worked in this very kitchen, although it's been remodeled a few times since."

She pushed aside her plate, got comfortable in her chair and so did he. And the conversation continued. He told her about how his great-grandmother had been a descendant of *Mitchelville,* the first free African American settlement in Hilton Head. He was surprised she had never heard of the historical settlement and spent the next hour enlightening her on South Carolina history.

She helped him load the dishes in the dishwasher and while doing so, she told him about her own ancestor who'd founded Claxton and how he had been a solder in the Union Army. It was the same regiment the movie *Glory* was based on.

By the time they climbed the stairs to go to their own bedrooms, he had to admit he enjoyed her company. He also had to admit he had learned some things about her. Like the fact that becoming mayor of Claxton had been a lifelong dream of hers. Clearly she still carried the pain of that defeat. The townspeople had let her down and the defeat had left her questioning her value and worth to a town she had lived in nearly all her life. It pissed him off the people she thought she knew and could depend on had done that to her.

He glanced over at her. "I need you well-rested tomorrow."

She frowned. "Well-rested for what?"

"Work. Because of you, I've gotten behind and need to get caught up."

"But what about the start of the interview? The sooner we begin the quicker we'll be through."

As they walked side by side, on occasion their shoulders brushed. He tried to ignore the pounding in his chest every time it happened. He stopped walking, deciding his chest needed a break. He turned to her. "That might be true, but I'm working against a deadline."

She stopped walking as well and lifted her chin. "So am I."

"And for some reason you assume yours is more important than mine?"

She had the good sense to look away. She was the one who needed the interview, so she was at his mercy. She looked back at him. "May I question you while you work?"

"No. When I work I concentrate on work." Although he fully expected while she was around, there would be a lot of time that he would be concentrating on her. After all, he was a red-blooded male and she was a woman. Yes, she was definitely a woman.

"Like I said, I suggest you get a good night's sleep. We work with the sea horses all day. When we get a break, then you can ask your questions."

With him leading the way, they began walking again. He glanced over at her and said, "And at some point, you'll need to return to the hotel for more clothes."

"I think what I have is sufficient."

"I don't. If you were interviewing anybody else would you rotate wearing the same thing every few days, even if they were clean?"

"No."

"Okay then. Besides, I'd like seeing you in a dress at some point."

She stopped walking. "Why?"

"You have great legs."

She glared at him. "That's sexist."

He chuckled. "No, that's being truthful."

They had reached the landing to the second floor. "And this is where we part, since I'm up another floor. I would walk you to your bedroom door but that's too much temptation. Like I said, tomorrow is going to be a busy day. Good night, Ainsley."

"Good night."

She turned and headed toward the guest room she'd been given. He knew she was still somewhat upset with him but, if truth be told, he was slightly upset with her, as well. He was going to be sleeping alone and after a night like last night, he thought that was a damn shame.

"Ainsley?" he called out to her.

She turned around. "What?"

"I suggest you stay in your room and not go moseying around tonight. If you do, busy day or no busy day, I won't be able to control my primal instincts. Let that serve as a warning."

"Warning taken," she said, then turned and kept walking and didn't look back at him.

Chapter 15

"Good morning, Winston. Isn't it a beautiful day?"

Winston's brow lifted when Ainsley all but breezed into the room, smiling in a way that showed her dimples. Why hadn't he noticed them before? Probably because when it came to him she rarely smiled. "Good morning. Your breakfast is warming on the stove."

"Thanks, and here is the list of questions," she said, placing a sheet of paper on the counter.

He sat there, sipping his coffee in between tugging in deep breaths while he watched her move around the kitchen, filling her plate and opening his refrigerator to grab a carton of orange juice. Why was she in such a good mood? Hell, he certainly didn't have anything to smile about. He had gotten very little sleep last night. Instead, he had lain awake, flat on his back while staring up at the ceiling remembering all the things he had done to his houseguest the night before. He'd thought putting her on the second floor was the ideal solution. But her scent had managed to penetrate all the way up to the third floor.

"You had to get up early in order to cook all of this," she said, joining him at the table. Instead of answering, he intentionally grunted. Maybe she would get the hint that he wasn't in a talkative mood.

"I woke up to the sound of the ocean and opened all the windows. It was wonderful. I envy you being able to do that. In New York…"

She continued to chatter away and he wondered what was going on with her. This was the most talkative she'd ever been around him. "Excuse me," he interrupted her.

She glanced over at him. "Yes?"

"What do you think you're doing?"

He knew her mind was probably struggling with the meaning behind his question, so he elaborated. "Why are you so mouthy this morning?"

She lifted her chin. "Just trying to be friendly."

"Don't bother."

She stared at him as she took a sip of her juice. "Evidently you got up on the wrong side of the bed."

"And evidently you got up on the right side," he said curtly.

Ainsley couldn't help wondering what his problem was. She had awakened this morning after a wonderful night of sleep with the resolve that she wouldn't do anything to tick him off. Bobby had called last night and when she'd told him Dr. Chambers had agreed to the interview, he had let out an excited shout. There was no way she could let down her boss and still expect to get back her old job.

She continued to eat her shrimp and grits. It was delicious. She'd tried the Southern cuisine one morning at the resort's restaurant, but it hadn't tasted as good as this. Winston was lucky to have had his grandmother and mother to teach him how to cook.

She glanced over at him. He was reading *The Wall Street Journal* off one of those e-reader devices, all but ignoring her. But there was no way she could ignore him. His strikingly handsome features made such a thing impossible. His mouth was firmly set and she wondered if it was something he was reading that didn't sit well with him or if it was her presence.

As if he felt her staring, he lifted his gaze to connect with hers. For several hot and tense moments they sat there and stared. Ainsley could feel a flutter that began in the pit of her stomach and was causing havoc between her legs. Suddenly, her mind was bombarded with memories of the times they'd slept together and how intense the lovemaking had been.

He broke eye contact with her, snapped shut his e-reader and stood. "Join me near the dolphin tank when you've finished breakfast."

She swallowed a deep lump in her throat as she watched him grab the sheet of paper off the counter before walking out of the kitchen.

What the hell is wrong with me? Winston wondered an hour later, glancing over at the doorway for the umpteenth time, waiting for Ainsley to appear. Each time he thought he heard the sound of her coming down the stairway, a funny sensation would seep into his stomach.

Why was he so antsy about seeing her? Maybe this whole arrangement of her staying here while she did the interview was a mistake. He thought he could tolerate her presence but he was finding it harder and harder to do so.

He was about to start his daily log of the sea horses when

his cell phone rang. He pulled it out of his back pocket, recognizing York's ring tone.

He clicked on the phone. "What do you want, whipped?"

"Stop calling me that, W."

"Why should I?"

"Because I'm not the only who dropped out of the Bachelor in Demand Club. So did Uriel and Xavier."

"Yes, but you're the most recent and you went down without a fight. You talked crap about not ever falling in love and the next thing I know you're sending out wedding invitations. And you claimed you never liked Darcy, at least that's what you told us. So, yes, bro, you are whipped."

"Fine, keep calling me whipped if you like. I see it as being extremely happy."

"Whatever." And Winston had to grudgingly admit whenever he'd seen York over the past ten months since his marriage, he seemed happy. Too freakin' happy. "And what do you want?" That was another thing that annoyed the hell out of him. Although York still called often enough, the conversations now seemed to be rushed. Like he had something better to do with his time than hang on the phone with his godbrother. Uriel and Xavier were the same way.

"Darcy wanted me to check to make sure we don't need to add a date by your name for next month's anniversary party," York said, breaking into his thoughts.

Winston drew in a deep breath. "You know how I operate. I'm coming alone. You're the one whipped. Not me."

"And you better hope it stays that way or I'll never let you live it down."

"Hey, don't worry about me. You don't know what you're missing. In a way I should be grateful. With you, Uriel and Xavier married off, that means more single ladies for me, Virgil and Zion."

"And I still say all three of your days are coming. Single

ladies don't like staying single for long. I can see the three
of you eventually falling in line."

Winston frowned. "Don't try putting a curse on us, man."

They talked for a few more minutes and when he glanced
up and saw Ainsley, he said to York, "Hey, I've got to go."

"Okay, but if you change your mind about bringing a
date, let me know or better yet surprise us."

"I won't be changing my mind and there won't be any
surprises. Goodbye, whipped."

He placed the phone back in his pocket. "I was beginning to wonder about you," he said to Ainsley.

She shrugged. "Thought I'd hang back a while."

"Why?" he asked, his brow furrowing.

"To give you time for that attitude adjustment you so
badly need."

He couldn't help but grin. "Aw, come on. Are you trying
to say I wasn't sweet as apple pie this morning?"

She laughed. "Trust me. You don't want me to be bru-
tally honest."

He had a feeling she could be. "I guess not." He looked
at her. "I see you found the shirt."

"Couldn't miss it when you'd left it hanging on my doorknob."

A smile touched his lips. "The job I'll be doing today can
get messy and I didn't want you to ruin any of your pretty
little blouses, so I gave you one of my old shirts."

"Thanks. I appreciate it. When do you think we can
squeeze in some interview time?"

He'd decided he wouldn't be rushed. "Not sure. We'll
play it by ear."

"All right."

He wasn't sure what was all right about it when at that
moment he was tempted to pull her into his arms and have
his way with her mouth. But it wouldn't stop there. He

wanted to make love to her until both their bodies eventually went numb.

"We might as well get busy," he mumbled hoarsely, not wanting to think about the fact that she was wearing his shirt and something of his was actually touching her skin.

A savage burn began spreading in his stomach, and disgusted with what little control he seemed to have with her, he walked off with her following in his wake.

Ainsley leaned over to glance into the huge tank that contained hundreds of different species of fish.

She then studied Winston and wished she wasn't focused on just how good muscle shirts looked on him, outlining what a well-built body he had. He was keying data into one of several laptops. The man was in his own zone, attentive and observant. He told her that he preferred working alone, but would allow interns from Savannah State College School of Marine Biology to assist him during the summer months.

Winston had set up several workstations that surrounded five huge aquarium tanks. One was filled with sea horses, another with several species of plants and fishes. There was a third that contained baby dolphins, a fourth with a family of turtles, starfish, sea squirts and tunicates and the fifth that was Lucy and Ricky's home. She could only identify the latter two because Winston had taken the time to point them out to her.

To say he was knowledgeable about sea life was an understatement. And before he'd gone into what she'd perceived as his don't-bother-me-now mode, he had identified the different fish species, as well.

She let out a deep sigh. Last night he'd made it seem as if he had plenty of work for her to do yet all she'd done was type data into a spreadsheet on the computer. With that finished and nothing else to do at the moment, she was ready to ask questions.

"Winston?"

"Yes?" He didn't even take the time to look up from the laptop.

"When did you know you were meant to do this?"

He stopped stroking his fingers across the laptop and glanced over at her. "When I almost died at fifteen."

His brusque matter-of-fact response made her gasp, and her muscles tightened at the thought of him almost losing his life. "You almost died?" she asked in low voice, making sure she'd heard him correctly.

"Yes. I had a lot of allergies while growing up and we weren't sure where they came from since no one else in my family is allergic to anything. When I was fifteen, I had an allergy attack that almost ended my life. In fact, the doctors sent me home from the hospital saying there was nothing else they could do."

Ainsley's hand flew to her throat. "They actually sent you home to die?"

"Yes. But my grandmother wasn't having any of that. She went by boat into Mitchelville to visit her mother…and to get a recipe for a homemade Gullah remedy that my great-grandmother promised her would work."

He paused for a moment and then said, "The recipe called for a lot of ingredients, including ground oyster shells and squid serum. Less than three days later I was back in school and I haven't had an allergic reaction to anything since."

"That's some testimony," she said, shaking her head.

"Yes, it is and I knew then the importance of sea life for medicinal purposes, and vowed to make it my life's mission to do research to find other uses, as well."

He leaned back in his chair. "For those who recall me having the illness growing up, it's easier to say I outgrew it than to go into a lot of details on how I was cured. Those closest to me know and that's all that matters."

Now she understood what drove him to do what he was doing. What had initially stirred his passion. At least his passion for his work. She glanced around. This was his world. The one he was most comfortable with. The one he chose to live in. She liked that. And as she was beginning to know him, unravel him layer by layer, she would even admit she was beginning to like him.

"This is your passion," she said softly.

"Yes, everyone has one. And from our conversation last night, I assume going into politics is yours."

She shook her head. "Not politics per se, just to follow in my ancestor's footsteps and become mayor of Claxton. But then I had my chance so that's one dream lost I won't worry about."

"There will be another opportunity some day when his term expires, Ainsley. And like I said, you're not a quitter."

She glanced down into the tank with all the fish, studied several of them before looking back at him. "No, but I'd need the people's support. Not sure I'll get it since I didn't this time."

"Fools, all of them," he said. "You would have gotten my vote."

She believed him. "Thanks. My opponent won by a landslide, which leads me to believe that even those who started out supporting me stopped doing so once that lie came out about me."

"The one about you being a stripper and not a dancer."

He hadn't asked but simply stated. There was no need to inquire as to how he'd known the specifics. "Yes."

He didn't say anything for the longest time, just continued to look at her for a few moments before turning back around to finish what he'd been doing on the laptop.

She glanced back into the tank. His questions had drummed up heartache that she wanted so much to forget. She still couldn't understand how people who'd known her all her life could believe the worst about her from a stranger.

"Come here a minute. I want to show you something."

She glanced to where he'd moved from the workstation to the tank that held the sea horses. "What?" she asked, coming to stand beside him and glancing over into the tank. She couldn't stop her body from responding to his closeness no matter how much she tried.

"The sea horses are in their last round of courtship. There will be a full moon tonight, which means they will probably mate," he said.

There was something in the way he said "mate" that started sensuous sensations rolling around in her belly. "Is it a gang bang or is it a one-female-for-one-male thing?" she asked.

He chuckled and she could practically feel his breath on her neck which made her realize just how close they were standing. "Um, like in most species, male sea horses can get rather possessive. And if the female approaches another male, her lover-to-be actually snatches her head to get her back in line. What he does is rather painful and usually it reminds her who she belongs to."

"Sounds like caveman tactics."

"Whatever you want to call it, it works."

"For a sea horse. I wouldn't try it if I were a real man."

"Probably not. Look."

He pointed out a group of sea horses and she watched as the female tried to swim away and a dominant male did exactly what Winston said he would do, snatch her head in a way that Ainsley knew had to be kind of painful. "Ouch."

He chuckled again. "You do what you have to do. And if you noticed, most of them are paired off now. Waiting."

"For what?"

"Tonight and the full moon. They always mate during a full moon."

She swallowed the lump in her throat. "And you will be here?"

"Yes. I have to document everything. The courtship, the mating, the pregnancy and delivery."

He took a step back. "Now I need to key information into the log. Then after feeding Lucy and Ricky, I'll be free."

She glanced up at him. "Free?"

"Yes, for the interview. I've gone over your list and the first five questions are doable today."

Just the first five? There were over thirty questions on that paper. Hopefully, he would allow time for more tomorrow. Otherwise, it would take forever to finish the interview. Although Bobby had told her to be thorough and take all the time she needed, she definitely saw spending too much time with Winston more of a liability than an asset. "Okay, we'll do the first five," she said, deciding not to push for more or he might retaliate by doing less. "And just so you'll know, I won't be here for dinner."

He lifted a brow. "You won't?"

"No. I need to go back to the resort and get some more things. I'll probably grab something to eat while I'm over on the other island. And I probably won't return until the morning. I don't see myself driving across that bridge late at night."

Winston didn't say anything, but for some reason the thought of her leaving Barrett Shores bothered him. It was only because he'd gotten used to her being here, he told himself. Moments later, he said, "Tell you what. I'll take you over to the island to get your things."

He could tell she was surprised at his offer. "You don't

have to do that. Besides, I don't want to take you from your work."

"No problem, and we can both grab something to eat. I'm not in the mood for cooking tonight anyway."

"Okay, thanks."

A smile touched his lips. "Then it's settled. After the interview I'll take you over to Hilton Head and while we're on the island we'll grab something to eat. And I know the perfect place."

Chapter 16

Winston had patiently sat in the resort's lobby and waited for Ainsley to return downstairs with her bags. He had convinced her that there was no reason to remain checked-in at the resort. It would take all the rest of her time in Hilton Head to go through all thirty of those questions. He was glad she had agreed.

After leaving the resort, they'd had dinner at Sharpie's, a Gullah restaurant in Mitchelville that was owned by one of his cousins. The aroma of steamed crabs and shrimp had greeted them at the door. He'd seen the surprised look in his cousin's eyes when he walked in. It was the first time he'd taken a woman to dinner there.

All through their meal he had forced himself not to stare over at her. The dress she'd changed into at the resort had been torture for him since the moment she had returned to the lobby. It was nothing as provocative as she'd worn that first night. It fact it was a beautiful blue shirtdress whose hem stopped just above the knee, but it showed off those gorgeous legs he'd wanted to see.

The moment she had stepped off the elevator at the resort, he had stood up and stared at her, flooded by memories of those same luscious legs wrapped around him while they'd made love. He had been grateful for the blazer he brought along due to the late evening chill. He'd clutched it in front of him to hide the way seeing her legs had made him hard.

Now dinner was behind them and they had just crossed the bridge to return to Barrett Shores. Ainsley had been quiet over the last twenty minutes and for a while he'd thought she'd drifted off to sleep. But whenever he had come to a traffic light and glanced over at her, he saw she was wide awake.

He had to admit their first interview session that day had gone well. Maybe because he'd known her questions beforehand. Or because the questions themselves had been easy, nonpersonal and about his work. They also covered the education to prepare him for the career he wanted and why he'd chosen to work under an alias. It would be news to everyone that Dr. R. J. Chambers was an alias but it wouldn't shock the academia world, since a number of his colleagues did the same thing. Most, like him, weren't seeking a name for themselves and preferred working without being pestered.

"I can't believe how easily you drove across that bridge," she said, interrupting his thoughts. "I held my breath the entire time."

He couldn't help but smile, imagining her doing that very thing. "I've lived here all my life and I can remember when my father and grandfather finished it."

"They built the bridge?"

"Yes, the state of South Carolina offered to replace it a couple years ago, but only if we sold the island to this developer. As long as it remained a private island it would be up to us to make the link."

"Before the bridge you got to Hilton Head by boat?"

"Yes, but Hilton Head isn't the only island around here, just the largest and most progressive since developers have all but taken it over. In a way it's sad because some of the people who'd lived here all their lives were forced to move away when property taxes became unaffordable."

She could hear the disappointment in his tone. "Your cousin seemed to be doing well with the restaurant."

"Yes, only because it's in Mitchelville, which has been declared a historical site thanks to the Mitchelville Preservation Project. The group is determined to keep the history and heritage alive. I'm a member and I know my grandmother and great-grandmother would be proud to know the history will continue to live on."

"And I'm glad, too."

She would be, he thought, not because she had a history maker in her own family with the first Ainsley, but because she came across as someone who believed in giving credit where credit was due. He'd noticed during the interview how she would highlight something he'd done in his studies that he hadn't thought twice about. But she had noted the importance of it.

"I still can't get over just how beautiful your home is," she said as they turned into the driveway and the house sprawled majestically before them with the crystal-blue ocean as a backdrop.

"Thank you."

He glanced up at the sky. Dusk would be rolling in soon and with it the full moon. He had a lot of work to do tonight. He parked the car beside the spot where he'd moved hers earlier that day. "I'll carry in your things and then it's back to work for me."

She looked up at the sky. "That's right. It's a full moon tonight. Mind if I observe, too?" she asked.

He could hear the excitement flowing through her voice. "No, I don't mind, as long as you're quiet. Too much noise will interrupt the process."

"Okay, I'll be quiet, I promise."

He wasn't sure if he believed her, given her propensity for being chatty at times. But he figured he'd take a chance. "All right, but I'm holding you to that promise."

"What's happening now, Winston?" Ainsley whispered. For the past few hours she had stood at the tank and watched the sea horses while Winston snapped pictures and intermittently logged data on his iPad.

"The male is offering his feeding bag to the female," Winston whispered back in a low tone. "Usually it takes a few hours to accomplish this because he does it over and over again, to make sure it's in place. The female will then dock part of her body over it. The male has the pouch."

Ainsley couldn't help but smile. "That's right. It's the male who gets pregnant."

She studied the sea horses some more. "Why are they changing colors?"

"The female is in the process of making eggs." He glanced up from his iPad over at her. "Similar to a female in the human species, she's at her hottest point during ovulation. Ripe and ready."

Why did his words cause heat to flush her face and blood to rush fast through her veins? "Is she?"

"Yes." He gestured to the tank. "Watch and see what happens next."

She broke eye contact with him and looked back over in the tank. The females were making eggs and then depositing them in the male pouch where he would fertilize them.

"This is simply amazing," she whispered, determined to keep her voice down.

"Yes, but not as amazing as when a man and woman mate. Sea horses do a lot of docking where for us it's a lot of thrusting."

Suddenly, an image flashed through her mind of all the thrusting he'd done inside her. She knew she needed to keep the topic of their conversation on the sea horses and not on men and women. "How long does it take for the male sea horse to become pregnant?"

"Immediately. Then it's a matter of the embryos growing to term, which takes three to six weeks."

He paused a moment and added, "It probably will make you happy to know scientific studies have concluded that the male actually experiences pain when giving birth."

A huge smile touched Ainsley's lips. "That does make me happy. At least some male species will know how it feels." She then thought about what else he said. "I hate I won't be here when the babies are born."

"Not babies, but sea ponies." And then he added, "You could always come back."

She glanced over at him, surprised. "Is that an invitation?"

He nodded. "Yes, I guess it is."

"Thanks."

Winston chuckled. "Although you might regret returning when you see what the male does at birth. After the pain."

She lifted a brow. "What does he do?"

"Nothing. Literally. As soon as the sea ponies are born, he leaves them, high and dry. To fend for themselves. The males don't have a maternal instinct in their body."

She turned back to look inside the tank where the females were still depositing eggs inside the males' pouches. "How sad."

"Yes, it is."

She was so engrossed in the process playing out before her that she didn't hear Winston coming to stand beside her until he touched her, startling her.

"I didn't mean to scare you."

She glanced up at him. "I guess I was preoccupied."

He nodded. "I need to record this," he said, holding up his iPad and videoing what was going on with the sea horses. Moments later, he said, "That does it for a while." He placed his iPad aside. "The only pitfall in watching sea horses mate is what doing so can do to you."

Her chest felt tight when she drew in a deep breath. His arms had accidentally brushed hers when he'd placed the iPad on the table. "And just what can it do?" she asked, not sure she wanted to know.

"I can only speak for myself, but it makes me want to mate as well under a full moon."

She felt her heartbeat quicken and the area between her legs throb. Meeting his gaze, she asked, "Does it?"

"You watched. You saw. Did it do anything to you?"

If he expected her to admit that it did, then he would be waiting a long time. She shrugged. "Not really."

"Liar."

She couldn't help but chuckle. "Why do you think I'm lying?"

"Because," he said, moving a step closer, "I've made love to you, several times. And the one thing I do know about you is that you're a passionate person. Just as passionate as I am. We don't just mate when we come together, we burn up the sheets, detonate our bodies in one hell of an explosion." He reached out and slipped a hand through her hair. "Do we?"

"Yes." He leaned down and began kissing the corners of

her mouth. His lips felt warm and firm, causing sensations to run rampant through her.

"I thought we agreed there wouldn't be any more sex between us, Winston."

"I didn't agree to anything and I definitely wouldn't have agreed to that," he whispered as he continued to kiss her jaw.

When she made an attempt to turn, he tugged on her hair to hold her head in place. An act of possession...like a male sea horse conquering a female. "You're not a sea horse, Winston," she murmured softly. "That act of possession won't work."

"You're right. I'm not a sea horse. I'm a man so I'm hoping that *this* act of possession will."

And then he captured her mouth in his.

A charge of adrenaline rushed through Winston's bloodstream the moment Ainsley touched her tongue to his. This shouldn't be happening again, but he was too far gone to do anything about it. Emotions he'd never had to deal with before were swelling up within him, making logical thought virtually impossible.

His mouth still clinging to hers, he lifted her off her feet and she automatically wrapped her legs around his hips. He moved to one of the workstations, his heart kicking up a beat with every step he took. He wasn't sure how long he could last. Her hardened nipples were pressing into his chest, making his breathing pattern irregular and his erection throb that much more.

He broke off the kiss and whispered, "Let's show those sea horses that when it comes to mating, they have nothing on us."

The moment he set her backside on the desk, they began going at each other's clothes. She tugged his shirt over his head and reached down to unhook his belt and jerk it through the hoops.

There seemed to be a hundred buttons to her shirtdress, and he couldn't control his fingers to undo them properly. "Aw, hell," he said, giving up and ripping the dress from her body. Staring into her shocked face, he covered her hands with his and murmured softly, "Don't be mad. I'll buy you a new one, I promise."

And then he leaned in to take her mouth again with a hunger that was driving him insane. He didn't understand why he needed his tongue to tangle with hers, needed to feel his bare flesh against hers, or why he needed to get inside her and experience again the feel of her inner muscles gripping him, pulling everything out of him.

He tightened his arms around her waist, drawing her closer to the fit of him. Breaking the kiss, he kicked off his shoes and removed his pants and briefs. He glanced over at her and watched her ease her panties down those gorgeous legs and toss them aside. She then took off her bra, leaving her as naked as he was.

His breath caught as his gaze roamed over her. Her breasts were beautiful. He thought that the first time he'd seen them and thought that now. At that moment words could not fully express how he felt or what he felt. But he was certain it went beyond pure lust. It was something he couldn't put a name to and at that moment didn't want to think about. All he knew was each and every time they came together was more powerful than the last.

"I need you," he muttered on a throaty groan. "I can't wait. I need you now."

Reaching up he lifted her hips, widened her legs, and her body arched to take him in. Her inner muscles contracted, gripping hard to his engorged erection. "So damn good," he hissed through his lips, tightening his hold on her when she curled her legs around him and held on.

It was a good thing because he began pumping into her, thrusting, jackhammering his way to her womb. It was as if he was not a returning visitor but in a place where he belonged. Heat was pounding in his groin and he was pounding her.

He felt Ainsley clawing his shoulders, digging in her fingernails. What should have felt like pain only felt like pleasure. Intense pleasure that triggered a need for more of her and he was determined to feed that need.

When she whispered his name on a fractured groan, his thrusts increased with a ferocity he couldn't seem to control. He leaned in close and kissed her, his tongue mating wildly with hers with raw hunger. He needed the connection of their mouths the same way their bodies were locked. And when he knew he was mere seconds from one hell of a climax, he released her mouth and stared at her, needing his gaze locked with hers when a massive explosion ripped through them.

He came and kept coming; his release seemed infinite, unending. And when she screamed his name he knew she was drowning in the same pleasurable waters as he.

But they would survive, to do it again and again

Sighing with pure contentment, Ainsley snuggled in Winston's arms while he carried her up the stairs. "Where are you taking me?" she asked drowsily. They'd made love twice near the sea horse tanks and she felt totally drained.

"To my bed."

She thought of all the stairs he would have to climb. "Put me down, I can walk."

"No you can't."

He was right, she couldn't. But still… "I'm no light-weight, Winston."

Instead of responding, he stopped and kissed her. What was there about being with him that made her feel secure and protected, even when they were at odds with each other? He had looked out for her, provided her with shelter, food and clothes, even when being stranded on his island had been her fault.

And there was another type of security she felt whenever she was with him, one she couldn't quite describe. But it had to do with how the warmth from his body seemed to spread right to hers, seeping through her skin to penetrate every muscle in her body. It made her feel wanted, needed and desired in a way she'd never felt before.

Her arms tightened around his neck as she kissed him back. And when he increased the pressure on her mouth, she responded by moaning deep in her throat to let him know how much she enjoyed his kiss.

She felt him lowering her to the steps while his hands began touching every part of her naked body, tracing a path over every curve, heating her naked skin.

"You know, I've never taken a woman on the stairs before, but I can't make it to my room just yet."

The moment her back touched a wooden step, his body straddled hers, and already parts of her were throbbing with need and a desire that she couldn't control. This was simply madness. Never had her body been stirred to such a feverish pitch, driven to this degree of primal lust.

"Tell me you want me again, as much as I want you, Ainsley."

She loved hearing him say her name in that deep, husky tone of his. "Yes, I want you again," she whispered, meaning every word. Later she would dwell on the how and why he'd gotten embedded under her skin, but for now, he wanted to take her again and she wanted to be taken.

The house was quiet except for the sounds of their heavy breathing but his seemed to stop when he slowly eased into her, cupping her hips, lifting them higher so he could go deeper. And when he began moving inside of her, not missing a beat, stroking her at a vigorous tempo, she tried hard not to scream when pleasure began overtaking her, driving her to the brink of satisfaction so intense she felt like any minute she might be taking her last breath. And then it hit. An explosion that she felt all the way to the bone, denying her the ability to hold anything back. Demanding her to test the strength and endurance of her lungs when she screamed his name.

"Winston!"

"I'm right here, baby. I feel you all the way," he whispered against her ear. "Literally."

And she knew there was no way he couldn't feel her when her muscles were clenching him the way they were. Then his body clenched as well and he tightened his hold on her hips, held them steadily in place when he continued to pound into her. And then she felt his hot, molten release shoot all the way to her womb.

They were mating.

Definitely not for the purpose it was intended, but for a sharing of pleasure so extreme all she could do was moan his name. And she liked the fluid sound of him moaning hers. Mating couldn't get any better than this.

"This is true mating, the real deal," he whispered, breathing the words softly. It was as if he had read her mind, had known her thoughts.

She glanced up and her eyes moved over his features, especially the dark eyes staring back at her. She tightened her arms around his neck. "Yes," she said, looking deeply into his gaze. "This is the real deal."

And then her body got primed for another orgasm and she knew at that moment it wasn't about just sex for her after all. Winston Coltrane had stolen her heart.

Chapter 17

Opening her eyes to the sunlight, Ainsley stretched languorously while sighing deeply. Never had she awakened feeling so exhausted yet at the same time feeling powerfully pleasured.

She shifted to her side to glance out the window, hearing the sound of the ocean. And then there was the heavy scent of the sea, something she was getting used to. She was beginning to love it here, too much. And last night had only added to her dilemma. Her heart had spoken and there was nothing she could do about the rendered verdict.

Winston Coltrane was something else, she thought as visions from the night before flashed through her mind. Starting at the sea horse tank and then culminating here in his bedroom…and she couldn't forget that stop in between. He'd said he'd never made love on the stairs. Well, neither had she. But she would do it with him again in a heartbeat.

Only him.

She glanced to where he'd slept beside her. She smiled at the thought. Actually they'd done very little sleeping. He was gone but he'd left a note pinned to the pillow. Ainsley pulled it off and read it.

Got plenty to do today, logging in all the details of last night...regarding the sea horses, that is. You'll probably want to rest up. Go ahead and sleep late. I'll be in the lab and when you get up we can cover the next five interview questions. I'll leave your break-fast warming.
WC

She held the paper to her chest thinking that other than her father—when she'd been twelve and her mother had gone to visit her sister, Aunt Rose, who'd had surgery—no man had ever kept breakfast warming for her. In fact, no man had ever prepared breakfast for her period.

She pulled herself up in bed, hugged her knees as she glanced around Winston's bedroom. Last night she'd been too drugged with lust to notice her surroundings. Today, in the brightness of a new day, she did. The room was huge, the furniture—which included the red maple California king bed she was in—was perfect. And the wall-to-wall window facing the ocean was simply breathtaking.

Easing out of bed she stretched her body again. She would take a shower, dress and then go down to the kitchen and eat the breakfast Winston had left for her. Before join-ing him near the tanks, she would take time to go over to-day's interview questions.

At the thought of seeing him again, she felt butterflies fluttering in her stomach. Yes, she had fallen in love with Winston Coltrane and there was nothing she could do about it but try to keep a level head and remember that although she might love him, the feelings weren't mutual.

Ainsley's scent reached him even before he saw her.

Winston glanced up from studying the liquid in the vial that he'd collected that morning and waited, his heart pounding like crazy in his chest, while at the same time a stream of desire was stirring in his groin.

How could he still want her with such intensity after all they'd shared last night? The way he'd taken her on the workstation near the tanks, the stairs and then later in his bed. He hadn't known there was that much desire in the world, but he was finding there was when it came to her.

He had awakened this morning and glanced over at her sleeping beside him. An inexplicable feeling of satisfaction had nearly overtaken him at seeing her there and in knowing after he took his shower, unlike that first night, she would still be there. She had no reason to flee.

In no hurry to move yet, he had lain there and watched her sleep, noting her breathing pattern and the way every once in a while the corners of her mouth would flinch. She had looked insanely beautiful lying there sleeping peacefully, and it had taken every ounce of control he had not to wake her, shift her body and slide right into it.

His mind was pulled back to the present when he heard footsteps outside the lab door. There was a soft knock and he said, "Come in."

She eased open the door and, the moment their eyes connected, he felt an immediate tightening of every muscle in his body. The sight of her practically burned his eyes when they raked over her. Her hair was different. She had pulled it back and twisted it up on her head. And she was wearing another dress—a flowered sundress with pockets this time—showing off her legs. When she smiled at him, he'd almost lost it then and there. She had such a radiant look about her. Unabashed beauty that nearly took his breath away.

"Hi," she greeted smiling over at him.

"Hi, yourself. You okay?" He needed to know. He had taken her hard more than a few times during the night.

"I am one-hundred-percent fine," she said chuckling. "If I was any better I wouldn't know what to do with myself."

"I can come up with several ideas," he said huskily.

"I'm sure you can. And I can come up with several myself. I bet it will prove dangerous for us to compare notes."

He laughed. "Probably." He placed the vial aside. "Ready for the next set of interview questions?"

"Only if you have time. I don't want to take you from your work," she said.

"No problem. Come on in and fire away."

"All right."

He watched her cross the lab, but stop when she noticed a framed picture on the wall. She stood there and studied it for a second and then asked, "Who are these guys with you?"

"My godbrothers." He rose from the stool and moved to stand beside her. "I'm sure you recognize me." And then he pointed out the others. "This is Uriel Lassiter, Zion—the youngest yet the tallest—and Virgil Bougard, Xavier Kane, and the one with the intense look is York Ellis."

"Nice-looking. All five of them."

He chuckled. "If you say so."

"The six of you are standing beside a NASCAR car. Is one of them a racer?"

"No, but a friend of ours, Bronson Scott, is and we usually get together and attend the races."

"Bronson Scott is a friend of yours? *The* Bronson Scott?"

"Yes, and before you get any ideas about an interview, Bron is worse than I am when it comes to protecting his privacy."

He moved back to his workstation and watched as she walked over to sit on a stool at one of the counters. She crossed her legs and his gaze followed the movement.

"First question of the day," she said, claiming his attention.

He glanced from her legs to her face. "Yes?"

"You're incredible in bed. Why?"

That question had certainly not been on the list she'd given him. He smiled, though, liking the fact she thought he was incredible in bed. He thought she was pretty damn remarkable in bed, as well. "That's an easy question to answer. If I was incredible, it was because of the woman I was with. She brought out the best in me. The kind of hunger I've never felt before."

He could tell from her smile that his answer pleased her. "Do you consider yourself a womanizer?"

"Depends on your definition of womanizer."

She uncrossed her legs and crossed them again. "A man who likes a lot of women."

He shrugged. "I enjoy women, but only one at a time."

He noted she wasn't taking notes which meant she would probably file away the answers in her mind somewhere. Then she pulled a notepad from one of the pockets of her dress and went back to the scripted questions. "So, tell me about this new drug you've developed…the one before the FDA. Only tell me what you're comfortable in sharing since it's still somewhat of a secret for now."

Not for long, he thought, thinking of the conversation he'd had that morning with the head honchos at Premier, the pharmaceutical company that had gained the number-one position worldwide. They'd made him an offer, one that almost made him fall on his face. "Okay, my formula will not only enhance a man's sex drive, but also his sex life more than one hundred percent with no side effects."

"No side effects?"

"None. In fact, one of the ingredients is proven to reduce high blood pressure and cholesterol levels."

"That's a huge claim. Has it been tested?" she asked.

"Yes, in a number of trials. Men whose ages range from early fifties to as old as ninety-five."

She nodded, writing down the information. "You know any of these men?"

He chuckled. "They're mostly anonymous. But there is one man that I do know personally."

"Who?"

"My father. But I prefer not seeing his name in print."

She stopped jotting notes in her notepad. "Your father?"

"Yes. And I have heard from a very reliable source— my mother—that Norjamin works. And according to my father's physician, he no longer has high blood pressure. Of course, my father had to do his part by shedding a few pounds, but the main thing is that Norjamin did what it is supposed to do and more."

"Winston, that's wonderful."

"Thanks. Would you like to take a look at some of the studies that were done?"

Her eyes widened as if he'd just offered her a huge chunk of Mt. Rushmore. "You'll let me take a look at them?"

"Just as long as you promise not to include any of it in the article without my permission."

"Yes, yes. I promise."

He got up and unlocked a file cabinet to pull out a huge stack of papers. "There's a lot of reading here, but I think you might find it informative."

"I'm sure I will. Do you mind if I sit here and start reading? Will my presence disturb you?"

"No." What he wouldn't tell her was that her presence was wanted and the mere thought of that bothered him. He never was the clingy type when it came to women. In fact, as far as he was concerned, out of sight meant out of mind.

However it wasn't that way with Ainsley. From the first time he'd seen her, he had become fixated with her whether he wanted to admit it or not. He had thought about her, dreamed about her, and when it came to making love to her, he was totally captivated. It was as if she was the only woman he wanted to think about making love to. Ever.

He glanced over at her. She was quiet, busily reading the documents he'd given to her, engrossed in her own world while he was engrossed in her. He'd never been this taken with a woman, no matter how good the sex was. And he was allowing her, a reporter, to read documents he normally guarded with his life. Why?

Okay, whatever it was, he was certain it would wear off eventually. The most important thing was to make sure he didn't get consumed by it. The last thing he wanted was getting whipped like three of his godbrothers. He was convinced there wasn't a woman alive who would make him think twice about settling down. Not in this lifetime. It would take an extraordinary woman to put up with his work habits, moodiness and sexual hunger. At least he knew Ainsley could handle one out of the three. Each and every time they made love, her needs had been on a level equal to his.

She must have felt him looking at her because at that moment she glanced up. "What?"

"I was just wondering how long it's going to take for you to finish all the interview questions."

"Why? Do you prefer I not be here?"

He couldn't help but smile at that. "No. I like having you here and you're welcome to stay for as long as it takes."

Her smile touched everything inside of him. "Thanks, Winston."

"You're welcome." She returned to reading the report

and he tried to concentrate on studying the contents in the vial containing serum from an Australian loggerhead turtle.

For the first time in a long time, he felt totally content.

"How am I doing so far?" Ainsley asked, putting the last ingredients into the bowl. She was trying to follow one of Winston's grandmother's family Gullah recipes and he was supervising. The fact that he was sharing the recipe with her was surprising in itself, but she would have to admit over the past few days there had been a lot of surprising developments.

"You're doing great. You season it to taste. Your taste. I doubt if you can go wrong with this."

Ainsley chuckled as she stirred up everything in the bowl. "Wanna bet? Like I told you, I am not a cook. I do better ordering out, but you make it look so simple and easy, I just have to try it."

"You're doing a great job. All you have to do is follow all the steps, season to taste and cook. No magic."

She wasn't so sure when he was in a kitchen. The man had all kinds of skills and cooking was one of them. She poured the mixture into a pan and placed it in the oven. "Okay, one hour at 350 degrees."

"That's right, and while we're waiting, I'll look over what you've written so far."

It was hard to believe how fast the days went by. She had finished all the interview questions, written the first draft and had presented it to him that morning to review.

"So far I like everything I've read, but I do have one problem with it," he said, leaning against the refrigerator.

"Oh? What?" she asked, slightly disappointed. She thought it was a good piece and had hoped he liked it with little, if any, changes.

"You're painting me as brilliant."

She couldn't help but smile. "You are brilliant. Do you know the impact of your medical discovery on the human population? You should be proud of yourself. I am if you're not."

"Yes, but the FDA has to approve it first, Ainsley."

"And they will. I read your report. You documented everything well." She had studied the report and seen the numbers. What he'd done had taken dedication on his part and it hadn't been cheap. According to him, in addition to grants he was able to obtain, his immediate family, godparents, godbrothers and his cousins from Mitchelville had all contributed to the Barrett Shores Research Foundation. The donations had not only been an act of love but also of strong support.

"But other than me painting you as brilliant, you liked it?" she asked, crossing her fingers.

He smiled. "Yes, I liked it. You did an outstanding job, although I was pretty difficult at times during the interview."

She returned his smile, remembering those times. They would start out with a pretty serious interview session and, halfway through it, they would be tearing off each other's clothes. "You weren't difficult, not really."

"I wasn't?" he asked, leaving his post by the refrigerator to come stand in front of her.

"No, I enjoyed the interview sessions. They were… intense. And you have to admit I did get through all thirty questions, eventually."

He chuckled as he reached out and twirled a strand of her hair around his fingers. "Yes, eventually."

She inhaled deeply, thinking just how perfect life could be if…

Her breath suddenly caught when she realized where her thoughts were going. Life was already perfect or getting there. With the article almost finished, she would eventually get back her job. That meant she would be leaving Barrett Shores to then leave Claxton to return to New York and be in her own little world again. She could do the plays, treat herself to days in Times Square and go dancing whenever she wanted. Life would be good. It would be perfect.

Who was she fooling?

"We got an hour to spare," Winston said huskily close to her mouth.

She looked up at him. "Do we?"

"Trust me. I know this recipe."

She eased close to him. "So what do you suggest?"

He used his finger to tip back her head and kissed the corners of her mouth. "What about a walk on the beach?"

She blinked. That wasn't what she'd thought he had in mind. "A walk on the beach?"

"Yes. Grab your jacket so we can go. We only have an hour."

"Oh, all right."

She turned to walk out the kitchen when he called her name. "Ainsley?"

She looked over her shoulder. "Yes?" She let her eyes graze over him. No man could wear a pair of jeans quite like him.

A crooked, naughty smile curved one side of his mouth. "I need more than an hour with you today...*that* way."

She couldn't help smiling knowing she had a lot to look forward to later.

Winston carefully eased from the bed and stood at the edge to glance down at Ainsley. The moonlight shining through the window cast streaks of light on her naked body. The entire room smelled of sex and he instinctively breathed in that scent. Her scent. One that had gotten to him from the first. Reeled him in and was still holding him tight.

He rubbed his hand down his face. What the hell was happening to him? Why had he begun feeling so vulnerable where she was concerned? She had been on Barrett Shores for almost two weeks now. Two mind-blowing weeks. And he would admit they had been the best two weeks of his life. Waking up with her. Going to bed with her. All those times in between. She would help him feed Lucy and Ricky each day and, once they covered the interview questions for that day, she would make herself useful by assisting him in the lab and inputting data into the system. And he'd let her look under his microscope to see things that interested him as a biologist. He'd even shared with her his desire to work on the Great Barrier Reef to further his studies on the Australian loggerhead turtles.

Then at night, every night, before they retired to bed, she would dance for him. It amazed him how agile her body was and no matter what dance she performed, she was simply beautiful. He even had a new appreciation for hip-hop. And after she finished each dance, she would take a bow then cross the room to curl up in his lap. He would hold her while thinking how some man would be lucky to have her as a permanent part of his life.

Sighing deeply he figured with a slight chill in the room that he needed to cover her instead of just standing there, ogling her naked body and getting an erection all over again. But at that moment he had a desire to see all of her and to try and understand. What was there about Ainsley St. James that had him tied in knots? Why was he wanting to share things with her that he normally didn't share with women? That part of himself he'd always kept closed off. But he had allowed her to cross the threshold beyond the door. Like today in his kitchen.

Not only had he let her in it, he had even shared one of his grandmother's recipes with her. And then they had walked the beach holding hands and later, by candlelight, they had eaten the dinner she had prepared. Candlelight, for crying out loud. What man did such nonsense except when he needed to make a score?

So here he was at 2:00 a.m. trying to figure out what the hell was wrong with him. And why he didn't want her to leave Barrett Shores when there was no reason for her to stay. She had finished the article and it was time for her to move on and for him to start thinking about all those offers that had begun rolling in.

But at that moment, all he wanted to do was think of her.

He moved to the window and looked out. Affairs started and affairs ended. Life went on. Nothing was forever. Nothing. Hadn't Caroline taught him that lesson well? But why had he allowed her—the ex of exes—to be the one to teach him anything? Caroline should have been the last person to leave a lasting impression on him. But she had, and the pain she'd caused him had been ingrained in him.

But not anymore, he thought, turning around and glancing at the naked woman stretched across his bed. Suddenly, a heavy weight seemed lifted from his shoulders. At that moment he knew why his emotions had been so damn confused lately. And at that moment he knew what it meant to be *whipped*.

He smiled. He would have even laughed, if doing so wouldn't wake Ainsley. But bottom line, he knew without a doubt what he was going through. He had fallen in love with the most gorgeous, sexy woman alive. Hell, no one could blame him.

He eased back into the bed with her, cuddling close to her, and his smile widened when she whispered his name while she slept. He knew he had his work cut out for him. She had a life that didn't include him and that was the life she intended to return to in a few days.

But he knew what he had to do. Somehow, he needed to get her to see that she belonged with him, just like he knew without a doubt that he belonged with her.

He needed more time.

More time to show her that his feelings for her had grown beyond the bedroom and that he wanted a future with her. He could just come right out and tell her, but she had no reason to believe him. Besides, he believed that actions spoke a thousand words.

Now that she had finished the interview, her plans were to leave the island this weekend. That gave him four days to change her mind.

Chapter 18

The next morning Ainsley looked over the rim of her coffee cup at Winston, surprised. "You want me to stay two more weeks?"

"Yes," he said, buttering his toast. "You did say you didn't have to officially report back to your office until the first week in March, right?"

That was if she had *her* office to go back to. Although she had kept her end of the deal by handing in her interview, Bobby hadn't fully kept his. Yes, she had a job at the paper, at the same salary, but that other woman was still occupying her office and writing her column. Bobby hadn't told her when that would end. He just said that it would eventually. Not having a definite date didn't sit well with her.

Still, she wanted to be settled in New York in the early part of February. There was her stuff to pack up at her parents' place in Claxton while spending some time with them before she left to clean and reinhabit her newly vacated condo. If she stayed longer here, it would make her time-table tighter. "That's right," she finally answered.

He nodded. "Two more weeks will give me time to do some things with you. I never got around to showing you the other side of the island," he said before taking a bite of his toast.

"You were busy."

He chewed his toast and paused to swallow it before saying, "Yes, but I'm going to have some free time on my hands for the next couple weeks. I want to go boating, crabbing on the beach, shrimping and scuba diving." He glanced over at her. "You do know how to scuba dive, right?" he asked.

She chuckled. "Wrong. I can swim but that's about it."

"Then I intend to teach you."

She had to laugh at that. "It would take me longer than a couple weeks to learn how to scuba dive."

"You'd be surprised what a good teacher I am."

She wouldn't, not really. He had taught her a number of things during the past two weeks, most of them in the bedroom. "Yes, but are you sure you want me hanging around for another two weeks? I would think you'd want your island back with just you and Charley."

"Would you believe me if I said that I enjoy your company?"

She would believe it, only because enjoying her company also meant enjoying her presence in his bed. He didn't have to say it but she knew that's what he really meant.

Really, girl, what else would he mean? Do you actually think that all those days the two of you hung out together here and those nights wrapped up in each other's arms meant as much to him as they did to you?

Part of her work had been in researching the real man behind the medical breakthroughs. Where there had been limited information on Dr. R. J. Chambers, there had been plenty on Winston Coltrane in the archives of several news-papers—especially the society section. Although he'd been lying low for a couple years doing research, his name had been linked to a stream of beautiful women. Some had tried real hard to get a ring on their finger and become the mis-tress of Barrett Shores. He was quoted more than once in several newspapers that he wasn't the marrying kind and intended to remain single forever.

"So…what about it? Think you can handle another two weeks of me and Barrett Shores?" he asked her.

She placed down her cup and picked up her fork. A smile touched the corners of her lips when she said, "Um…I love it here and you really aren't so bad."

He chuckled. "Glad to hear that. Does that mean you're staying?"

She sighed knowing if she decided to stay that meant eighteen more days. Shouldn't she leave now before she got any deeper into emotions she had no right to feel? But then all she had to do was look at him and her heart would go pitter-patter, letting her know that she wanted that addi-tional time with him. At least he wanted her and wanted to be with her. She needed those two weeks. And then when she left here, she would be able to accept a love that couldn't be. She would have closure.

"Yes," she finally said. "I'll stay two more weeks."

The days flew by but Winston was determined to make each one count for the both of them. Every morning upon waking, they would walk on the beach and talk, learning more about each other and sharing things that he'd never shared with any woman. He told her about the Bachelors in Demand Club, wanting her to know his initial dedication to it, so when he eventually told her that he was getting out of the club, she would understand the depth of his love for her.

After their walks on the beach, they would return and prepare breakfast. Together. He had gotten used to her working alongside him in the kitchen, even if she was only handing him the ingredients he needed. Then she would assist him in the lab where he would tell her more about his work with the turtles and his desire to one day set up a sanctuary near the Great Barrier Reef.

And now he was down to the wire. His heart cringed when he thought about their time together coming to an end. They were down to four days and he was determined not to let her leave Barrett Shores without telling her how he felt. Tonight was it and he had a big evening planned for them.

He wanted to take her someplace special and decided the perfect place would be where they'd met—the Sparrow.

The surprised look on Grady's face when they walked in was priceless. He pulled Winston aside the first chance he got. "Man, you did it. You said you were claiming her that night. Evidently things went down just the way you planned."

Winston darted a glance around the club in case Ainsley had returned from the ladies' room. He turned back to Grady. "To be honest, things didn't go down as I planned."

Grady looked surprised. "They didn't? But you're here with her now."

"Yes," he said smiling. "I hadn't planned on being so taken with her, but I am. I intend to marry that woman… if she will have me."

Grady stared at Winston as if he'd suddenly grown horns out from his head. "You let a woman do that to you, man? What kind of hex has she got you under? What—"

"No hex and I'm in my right mind, trust me," Winston said laughing.

Grady gave him a look that indicated he wasn't so sure.

"Well, I'd like to be a fly on the wall when you explain things to Virgil and Zion."

Winston sighed deeply. He would deal with those two godbrothers later. He was about to respond when he saw Ainsley returning. "We'll talk more later."

"Okay. And man, she still looks hot," Grady said with a huge smile on his face before walking off to tend to a customer. "And if I weren't a married man—"

"You would still do nothing. You love your wife too much," Winston said, watching Ainsley head back over his way. He felt a deep pounding of love in his heart. "And now I know the feeling."

Ainsley knew this feeling all too well.

The desire to make this night count. With so few left, each night had become special, precious.

When they returned to Barrett Shores after dinner, she decided to make this a night to remember for her and Winston. They had enjoyed a wonderful meal and had danced to her heart's content. Although she had taken pleasure in dancing to the sounds of hip-hop, Motown and disco, she had relished the slow dances the most, when he had held her in his arms, whispered naughty things in her ear and ground his body against hers, letting her know just how much he wanted her.

When she entered his home, she barely made it across the threshold before he pulled her into his arms. From the hard feel of his erection, she knew he still wanted her.

And she wanted him.

"I going to take you hard," he murmured in a raspy voice close to her ear, already easing down the zipper to her dress.

"I going to take you hard as well," she warned, reaching for the buttons on his shirt. She saw the dare of a smile on his face, those dimples that could kick her heart into overdrive.

There was no time for talk and they wasted no time in undressing each other, tossing clothes all over the place. The one and only thing Ainsley could think about was that she needed this, the memories of being here with him and of a moment in time she would not forget.

Within seconds they were flesh to flesh, skin to skin, heat to heat in a way that sent an urgent need all through her bones. She reached out, took his hardness in her hand, gloried in it, felt how the head throbbed beneath her fingers and how the bulging veins felt pressed against her skin.

Likewise he slid his hand between her legs, testing her readiness, and he gave her that oh-so-sexy smile again when he found her wet already. What had he expected?

She would have asked if her mind wasn't suddenly snatched from logical thought when his fingers slid inside her, delving deep between her legs. "You're hot, baby. Moist and…"

Releasing one of his fingers he placed it to his lips, licked, tasted and said, "So damn sweet."

Ainsley tightened her hold on his erection, rubbed her finger gently over the head and smiled when pre-release touched her finger. She brought it to her lips, sucked her finger hard, then said, "Aah…damn good."

As if her words triggered an intense primitive urge within him, he reached out, grabbed her by the waist and lifted her up, cupped her backside firmly and plunged inside her. His tongue echoed the action, invading her mouth.

Invasions, she thought, had never been sweeter, and she wrapped her legs around his hips as he continued to pound into her. Her mind became a turbulent vortex of sensations as he spread apart her legs to go deeper. He was a man losing control and she was a woman who'd already lost it. That was evident by the way she was returning his kiss, with a hunger, need and greed that could not, would not be denied.

Her skin felt hot, and she could feel his fingers move all over her, igniting flames across her skin. She felt herself being lowered—to what she wasn't sure—as he pulled away from her mouth and captured a nipple, sucking hard. She suddenly felt overwhelmed and lost as one erotic sensation after another assaulted her senses.

When she felt a soft cushion behind her back, she realized she was on the sofa. How had they gotten from the front door across the room with their bodies still joined? All she knew was that she was now flat on her back and Winston was on top of her, thrusting in and out of her.

Too much was too much and she cried out, calling his name when her body exploded in one hell of an orgasm. He was right behind her and she felt his hot release at the same time a guttural groan was torn from his throat. He tightened his hold on her, as if he needed their bodies to remain locked tight, unmovable, for a minute. Then another minute. And another.

Moments later, still intimately joined, he shifted their positions to where they faced each other. Instinctively, she tucked her head under his chin, took a deep breath of his scent and slowly closed her eyes. She wished she could stop the passing of time but knew she couldn't. So she cuddled closer knowing the next four days was all she had.

At that moment she heard her cell phone go off. It was close to ten o'clock. Usually she wouldn't get a call this late.

"You want to get that?"

She glanced over at Winston. A part of her wanted to say no, she didn't want to get it, because she didn't want to leave his arms, but then she figured she had better. "Yes. It might be important."

He released her and helped her up. She crossed the room

to her purse, trying not to notice all the clothes they'd gotten out of moments earlier. Her phone had stopped ringing and the caller had left a voice mail. She furrowed her brow when she saw the call had come from an unknown number with a Claxton exchange. She listened to the voice mail.

"Ms. St. James, this is Marv Lattimore, president of the Claxton Community Council. Not sure if you heard the news report but..."

When the voice mail ended, she clicked off the phone. Stunned.

"Ainsley? Is everything okay?"

She glanced across the room. Winston was still lying naked on the sofa and staring at her with a concerned look on her face. She couldn't shake off the significance of that phone call and how it could change her life forever.

"That was the president of the Community Council in Claxton. The mayor-elect, the man who beat me in the primary in November, was ousted from office on corruption charges. They will be holding a special election for his replacement in a week and will support me in taking his place."

He didn't say anything for a minute as he continued to stare at her. Finally he asked, "What are you going to do?"

What was she going to do? At one time she thought being mayor of Claxton and following in her ancestor's footsteps was all she wanted. But now...

"Ainsley?"

She drew in a deep breath, searched his eyes. For one heart-sinking moment she was hoping to see a sign...of what? That maybe...

She shook her head, knowing she had to be realistic. Winston didn't love her, she knew that. At least going back to Claxton and becoming mayor meant she would be too busy to reflect on the one man she couldn't have.

Swallowing the lump in her throat, she said, "Considering that call, I need to leave for Claxton first thing in the morning."

He nodded slowly. "Being mayor is what you want?"

Ainsley took a deep breath and said, "Yes. That's what I want."

Chapter 19

Winston had pulled the T-shirt over his head as he moved toward the kitchen. Suddenly Charley sounded. *"Visitor on property."*

Winston's heart kicked up several beats when he paused. Ainsley had left four days ago. Had she returned? "Identify, Charley."

"The handsomest of you all. York."

Winston rolled his eyes. Of course York had programmed Charley to announce him that way. Switching his direction, Winston moved toward the front door. He didn't have to wonder what had brought York to his doorstep. Winston hadn't been in the mood to take calls since Ainsley had left Barrett Shores and York was checking to see if he was alive or dead.

He was alive but inside he felt dead.

He opened the door and paused in the doorway, watching York get out of the car. Four days ago he had stood in this same spot and watched Ainsley get into her car and drive off the island forever. And that was the day a part of him had died inside.

Perhaps he should have told her how he felt. But what would that have accomplished if she didn't love him back? Besides, that call was giving her a chance to fulfill her dream and he couldn't stand in her way. He would never stand in her way. She wanted to be mayor of Claxton and now she would be.

He looked past York to the ocean while thinking that he would be the first to admit that those weeks Ainsley had spent here on the island with him had been the best days of his life. And he would always believe they'd forged a connection that had gone far beyond the bedroom.

"You look like hell."

He raised a brow at York's observation. So, okay, he hadn't shaved in a few days. But he had showered, brushed his teeth, combed his hair and put on clean clothes. So where was York going with this?

"Good seeing you, too, York."

York reached him, came to a stop, searched his face and frowned. "The hairy look doesn't become you."

"What brings you this way?" he asked, ignoring York's comment.

"You know what brings me this way. You weren't answering your phone and you know our agreement."

Yes, he knew their agreement. They stayed in touch and if one deliberately went out of the loop there had to be a reason. "As you can see, I'm fine," Winston said.

"Uh-huh." York walked past him into the house. "Hello, Charley."

"Hello, magnificent one."

York smiled. "Smart security system you have."

"Whatever."

York slowly glanced around, with that always-on-the-alert look on his face. He brought his gaze back to Winston. "Why do you look like hell, W, and why is this place drenched with the scent of a woman?"

"We need you to make a decision, Ainsley. Do you want to run for mayor or not?"

In a conference room at city hall, Ainsley glanced around at the six men and three women sitting at the huge table. She had arrived in town four days ago and they'd been certain she was ready to run on the ballot uncontested. A part of her had thought the same thing. But then she'd surprised the council by saying she needed time to think about it. One of the members, Madeline McCray, had even asked what there was to think about.

It was time she told them, as well as the decision she'd made.

"From the time I was a child growing up here in Claxton," she began saying, "I wanted to follow in the footsteps of the first Ainsley St. James and be this city's mayor. To work hard for every single person living here."

She paused a moment and then continued, "I thought my time had come when I threw my hat into the ring. I was convinced this was the job for me, that my town needed me. I had great ideas for moving Claxton forward, bringing in change everyone could agree with and working with all the townspeople to retain those small-town values we all love. But then, in stepped my opponent and all of you stopped believing in me and began believing lies about me that his campaign fabricated. Some of you even approached me about dropping out of the race to give him an uncontested win." She noticed the look of shame on a couple faces and in a way was glad for that.

"But we found out what he accused you of wasn't true,"

Madeline McCray said. "Last week I went to that club in New York myself and spoke to the owner. He remembered you, said what a hard worker you were and verified that you hadn't been a stripper but a dancer."

Ainsley stared at the woman. "You went to New York and talked to my former boss?"

"Yes," Madeline said smiling. "After what happened with Luis, this town didn't need another scandal on our hands, so we had to be absolutely certain of exactly what you did while working at that club."

"I told all of you what I did, but you still didn't believe me?" Ainsley asked calmly, refusing to let them disappoint her anymore. She looked down for a minute, studied her entwined hands and remembered what Winston had once told her. *When someone believes in you, there's no need for further doubt.*

Ainsley lifted her head and glanced around the room into the faces of people she had known all her life. They hadn't believed in her…but Winston had. Without any doubt she knew her decision was the right one for her.

"I suggest you look to see if someone else is interested in being your mayor." There was shocked silence around the table but at the moment Ainsley couldn't have cared less about their reaction.

"And you aren't interested?" Marv Lattimore asked while a number of council members exchanged stunned glances.

"Not anymore. The fact that you all still felt the need to check out my story even though I said it wasn't true lets me know you just don't fully believe in me." Ainsley stood. "In that case, I'm not going to be the right person to lead this city. And I wish you all the best in your selection process. I'm sure there's a candidate you'll believe in out there."

She then turned and walked out of the room.

* * *

"If you think you can stare me away, forget it," York said, easing down in the chair opposite from Winston who hadn't stopped glaring at his godbrother since he'd arrived. "So get it out. Who is she?"

Winston didn't say anything for a moment and then leaned back on the sofa, switching his gaze off York to look out the window. "Doesn't matter anymore."

"You look like shit, so I think it does."

It was on the tip of Winston's tongue to say he only looked like he felt. He turned back to York who raised a brow in what Winston recognized as a stand-off challenge. This particular godbrother could be a pain in the ass when there was something he wanted to know, which made Winston pity anyone who'd come up against York during his NYPD days.

"Her name was Ainsley St. James and she interviewed me for *The New York Times.*" He watched York's sharp dark eyes show signs of surprise and understood. He'd never allowed himself to be interviewed before.

"And…"

He should have known York was not going to let that be the end of it. So he decided to be completely honest. "And I became totally whipped."

If he expected amusement, he didn't get it. Instead York leaned forward with a serious expression on his face. "I think you need to start from the beginning."

Winston wasn't sure why he began talking, telling York everything. Maybe he needed to relive the moments for himself to make sure they had happened or maybe because hearing it allowed him a chance to treasure what had been and to accept what he now felt.

"And you let her walk away?" York asked when he'd finished.

Winston rubbed his hand down his face. "What else was I supposed to do?"

"Tell her how you felt."

"Why? It would not have changed anything."

"You don't know that."

York was right, he didn't. But he had refused to take the chance of getting hurt all over again. "Doesn't matter. I've made plans."

York lifted a brow. "What sort of plans?"

"I got a call yesterday. I've been offered the opportunity to set up a marine sanctuary on the Great Barrier Reef for the next three years. So maybe things worked out between us as they should have."

Even while he'd said the words, pain had stabbed deep at his heart because he knew that no matter where he went or what he did, Ainsley had made herself a permanent part of his existence and he wasn't going to forget her that easily.

"I see," York muttered breaking into his thoughts. "I've never known you to be a quitter, W."

Winston chuckled derisively. "And you've never known me to be whipped, either, so that goes to show that strange things can happen," he said, his mouth forming into a grim line.

Winston stood. "I'm about to have lunch and you're welcome to join me, but the subject of Ainsley St. James is a closed subject from here on out."

Not waiting for York to make a comment, he walked off toward the kitchen.

A week later Ainsley was back in New York and joining Tessa for dinner as they celebrated her return.

"So what are your plans now?" Tessa asked as she took a sip of her wine.

Ainsley smiled over at her friend and saw her worried

expression and felt the need to assure her that everything would be fine. "I got a call from Bobby a couple days ago and everything's final. Not only do I get back my old job but I'll be writing the column again in three months. The big brass liked the article I did on Winston which comes out in Sunday's paper."

Ainsley took a sip of her own wine and inwardly prepared herself for the question she knew Tessa would ask. She had eventually told her best friend everything. How she had fallen madly in love with Winston and knowing her love wouldn't be reciprocated, how she had left Barrett Shores after getting Marv Lattimore's call with the intent of not looking back. She'd had so much disappointment in her life lately, she didn't need anymore.

"And you haven't changed your mind about not reconnecting with Winston Coltrane?"

"Nope, it's for the best."

"You know I don't agree with you about that," Tessa said. "You let me read the draft of that article. Winston Coltrane is a very private man, yet he allowed you to spend time with him and get to know him as few people would."

She waved off Tessa's words. "It was only about sex… for him."

"How can you be so sure? What are you waiting for? Some sort of sign indicating otherwise?"

Ainsley chuckled. "A sign would be nice, but I'm not holding my breath for one. I can't live in the past. I have to move on. If nothing else, losing that election has taught me not to assume anything. Had Winston wanted me to stay, he would have said so."

Wanting to change the subject, Ainsley began talking about some of the decorating ideas she'd considered now that she'd moved back into her apartment.

In the middle of her explanation, Tessa interrupted her.

"Don't you dare turn around now, but three of the most handsome guys I've ever seen just walked in." Seconds later Tessa's lips formed a disappointed frown. "Forget it. They're all wearing wedding bands."

Ainsley nodded. Not that she was interested, no matter how good they looked. When they stepped in her line of vision as the waiter led them to their table across from hers, she couldn't help but agree with Tessa. They looked good. She didn't want to stare but something about them— all three of them—was familiar. She was certain she would have remembered them if they'd met. So where…?

It hit her when one of the men noticed her staring and glanced at her with an intense look on his face. That intense look gave him away because she'd seen it before—on the framed photograph hanging on the wall in Winston's lab. There was no doubt in her mind that these men were three of Winston's five godbrothers. She nervously broke eye contact with the man and took a sip of her wine, wishing it was something stronger.

"You okay?" Tessa asked her.

She swallowed and glanced over at her friend. "Yes, why do you ask?"

"Because you were staring at that guy and he was staring back. Do you know him?"

Ainsley nervously placed down her glass. She might have recognized him but she was certain he didn't know her. "No, I don't know him personally but I've seen a picture of him as well as the other two."

Tessa lifted an arched brow. "You have? Where?"

"Winston's place. They're his godbrothers. He has five of them."

"Five?"

"Yes, it's a long story."

"I can't wait to hear it. And you're sure that guy doesn't

know you, because he's still looking. He whispered something to the other two and now all of them are staring at you."

Ainsley hoped Tessa was wrong. She was certain those men didn't know her.

"Uh-oh," Tessa said with barely moving lips. "I hate to tell you this but that man—the one who was staring you down—has gotten up and is headed this way. And you're sure the two of you have never met?"

"Positive."

Seconds later she held her breath when the man stopped at their table. She looked at him and he stood there, staring at her with that same intense look. She cleared her throat. "Yes, may I help you?"

"Evening, ladies. I apologize for disturbing your meal," he said. He then turned his full attention to Ainsley. "But I was wondering if perhaps your name is Ainsley St. James?"

Chapter 20

"And just who wants to know?" Tessa answered curtly before Ainsley could get a word out.

The man switched his gaze to Tessa and gave her an indulging smile. "I do. I'm York Ellis," he said presenting his hand to Tessa.

Ainsley saw her friend softening under the man's smile. "And I'm Tessa Spencer."

"Nice meeting you, Tessa." He then turned his attention back to Ainsley.

Wondering how he knew who she was, she offered the man her hand. "Yes, I'm Ainsley St. James. You're one of Winston's godbrothers. He has a picture of you guys on the wall in his lab. We've never met so how did you recognize me?"

"From a picture, as well."

At the lifting of her brow, he added, "On his refrigerator. It was taken of you on the beach."

Ainsley's stomach tightened and she picked up her wine to take another sip. She remembered the day Winston had taken that picture during the last week of her stay on Barrett Shores. They had spent an entire day on the beach and she'd been wearing a very provocative bikini. She'd been stretched out on a beach towel and he'd called her name. When she had glanced up he had snapped the picture on his iPhone. She hadn't known he had even downloaded it. And he had placed it on his refrigerator? More sensations flipped her stomach at the thought of what that could mean.

"I'm surprised to see you in New York," York said interrupting her thoughts.

She glanced back at York. "Where else would I be? I live here."

He shrugged his massive shoulders. "Winston mentioned you had become mayor of some town in Jersey."

She reached out for her glass. "I turned the town down."

"Does Winston know that?"

No, she wanted to scream. *Mainly because he wouldn't care one way or the other. It wasn't that sort of relationship.* "Probably not," she heard herself say. "I haven't spoken to him since I left Barrett Shores."

"Well, I can remedy that," York said smiling. "Just so happens Winston is arriving in town later today to attend the anniversary party for me and my wife tonight. I'd like to invite you." He shifted his gaze over to Tessa. "The both of you."

Ainsley was surprised by the invitation. First of all, she didn't really know the honorees so she would feel out of place, and second, she didn't feel comfortable going to a party Winston would be attending. Why on earth would York think he would want her there?

"Thanks for the invitation, but I already have a date tonight," she heard Tessa say.

Ainsley released an inward sigh of relief. If Tessa couldn't make it, that meant she certainly wouldn't go. There was no way she would show up by herself.

York evidently thought otherwise. "Sorry to hear that, Tessa, but I'm hoping you will still come, Ainsley. Winston will be glad to see you."

She wondered how he assumed that. "Thanks for the invite but I can't come to the party. I won't know a living soul there. And it would be awkward, especially if Winston brings a date."

York chuckled. "We're a friendly group and you won't have to worry about Winston bringing a date. He never does."

"That's all the reason I shouldn't attend. He might not want me there."

"He'll want you there, trust me."

Ainsley nervously nibbled on her bottom lip. She wanted to trust York, although she really didn't know him. The only thing she knew was that he was like a brother to the man she had fallen in love with.

She glanced over at Tessa and her best friend smiled and then placed a hand on hers. "This sounds like the sign we were talking about earlier, Ainsley. Go for it. What do you have to lose?"

If only you knew... She glanced back up at York, her decision made, and she hoped it was the right one. She *would* go for it. "All right. Please give me the address of the party."

York's smile widened. "It will be in my home and I'll send a car for you around six. I just need your address."

Ainsley gave it to him. "Thanks, and if you don't mind, I'd like to introduce you to two of my godbrothers who're in town for tonight's affair, Uriel Lassiter and Xavier Kane," York said smiling.

"All right."

She watched as he motioned for the other guys to come over and at that moment, she couldn't help wondering if perhaps she'd made a mistake in agreeing to attend that party.

"So what have you been up to, W?" Virgil Bougard asked, taking a sip of his wine.

Winston knew Virgil would be the last person to whom he could tell what he'd been doing. He'd probably freak out to know Winston had joined the "whipped" team. Only difference was that U, X and Y had managed to snag the women who'd captured their hearts but he'd let his lady-love get away. He wondered how she was doing as mayor of a town that, as far as he was concerned, didn't deserve her loyalty.

"W?"

He blinked, realizing he hadn't answered V's question. "Busy as usual but I did take time out to do that interview with *The New York Times*."

"And how did that turn out?"

"Okay. The article will appear in tomorrow's paper." When Zion and Uriel walked up, he told them of his plans to move to Australia to work for the next three years.

"Man, that's great and I know for you it's a dream come true," Uriel said smiling. "Congratulations."

Zion and Virgil offered congrats, as well. "I suggest we split this party early," Virgil said, his eyes gleaming with mischief. "There's a gentlemen's club not far from here and tonight is when strippers are featured for entertainment… if you know what I mean." He then glanced over at Uriel. "Sorry, you can't join us, with you being happily married and all," he said with a grin.

Winston took another sip of his drink. He might be leaving the party early but he wouldn't be going to see any woman strip off her clothes. The last thing he wanted was to think about making love to any woman other than Ainsley.

He was about to ask Zion how he liked being back in the States when Virgil let out a low whistle. "Um, I take that suggestion back. I think I'm going to hang around to get to know that woman who just walked in."

"No, bro, you're going to have to stand in line behind me," Zion said chuckling.

Not even curiosity made Winston look over his shoulder at the woman his two godbrothers were fixated with. Instead he said, "I need some fresh air. I'll be out on the balcony." He then walked off.

"Hello, you must be Ainsley. I'm Darcy Ellis, York's wife," the woman who opened the door said smiling.

"Yes, I'm Ainsley and I appreciate the invitation."

"The pleasure is mine and York's," Darcy said. "Let me take your coat."

Ainsley handed Darcy her coat and a waiter was there to take it away. "That's a beautiful outfit, Ainsley."

"Thank you, and you have a beautiful home."

"Thanks. York had a bachelor pad and I owned a place half this size so we decided to purchase something of our own that would fit both our needs," Darcy said smiling.

Ainsley released a deep sigh. All the way over she had struggled with the temptation of asking the driver to turn around and take her back home. She had so many "what ifs" to deal with. What if Winston had brought a date after all? What if he got upset at seeing her here among people he considered as family and friends? What if the people weren't as friendly as York had claimed they would be?

She knew at least she could dispel her fears of the latter when the gorgeous woman smiled brightly at her and tucked her arm in hers as she led her away from the door.

"Any friend of Winston's is a friend of ours. We're all family," Darcy said.

Ainsley could see that as they came to a stop in front of two other women. "You probably got the chance to meet the two guys who were with York earlier today," Darcy was saying. "Now I want to introduce you to the women who have to put up with them," she said jokingly.

"Hi, I'm Ellie Lassiter," an attractive woman smiled and said.

"And I'm Farrah Kane," the other attractive woman said. "I just love that dress. Winston is going to love it, too, when he sees you in it."

Ainsley hoped so. As soon as she and Tessa had left the restaurant, they had gone shopping. Ainsley had known this dress was hers the moment she'd seen it. Winston had said he liked seeing her legs. Well, she hoped nothing had changed because she was wearing a red sleeveless mini-dress with ruffles at the hem and a black belt that emphasize her small waist.

"Ainsley, glad you made it," York said smiling as he came up to join them.

She returned his smile. "Thanks for sending the car for me."

"No problem," he said glancing around. "Winston was here a few minutes ago. I wonder where he's taken off to?"

"He's stepped out on the balcony," Uriel said as he and Xavier also came to join the group. "But I'm sure he'll be glad to know you're here," he added.

Ainsley wondered why he was so convinced that Winston wouldn't have a cow when he saw her. At that moment five other men joined them.

"Aren't you going to introduce us to your friend, Darcy?" the one Ainsley knew to be Virgil asked.

Darcy shook her head. "You guys are bad. You all have radar that beeps at the sight of a beautiful woman," she admonished.

Ignoring the comment, York leaned over to Ainsley and whispered for her ear only, "I'll let Winston know you're here."

He then walked off as Darcy began making introductions. Two of the men Ainsley remembered from the photograph on the wall in Winston's lab. Winston's godbrothers. She wanted to pinch herself at the thought that she was in the same room with Zion Blackstone, the world-famous jeweler. The other three men were brothers from Phoenix—Tyson, Mercury and Gannon Steele.

She couldn't help but smile as they tried flirting with her. But the one man she wanted to see was nowhere in sight.

Winston stood on the balcony and looked out into the night. York and Darcy owned a brownstone on the Upper East Side of Manhattan—a ritzy area near Central Park and the Metropolitan Museum of the Art. It was the second week in February. The temperature was twenty degrees and snow was predicted for the coming week, yet he barely felt the cold. His thoughts were focused on the memories he hadn't yet let go of, memories of the days Ainsley had spent with him on Barrett Shores.

Even now he could vividly remember those late nights and early morning hours when they would make love to the point of exhaustion. And how they would share breakfast together, walks on the beach and dinner, and then how she would dance for him in those intensely private moments they had. He was convinced it was when she had been dancing for him that he'd realized just how much he loved her. And later that same night while making love, he had reached the conclusion that he didn't want her just as a sex partner, but that he wanted Ainsley as a life partner, to share his life forever.

So why are you standing out here in the cold while she's tucked somewhere in the warmth enjoying her role as Madam Mayor of Claxton, New Jersey? Didn't she deserve to know that those days and nights meant something to you? Shouldn't she be the one to decide how she wanted her future to pan out? Why did you make the decision for her? What if she would have decided a life with you was worth more than a life as a mayor? What if...

He drew in a deep breath, tired of wondering and not really knowing. They had shared an intense affair and it was during some of those times that he'd felt so connected to her that he was certain she had felt the same emotions for him as he was feeling for her. But they'd never talked about a future, never discussed anything beyond what they'd been sharing on his island. Maybe they should have. Was it too late?

He glanced at his watch. As far as tonight was concerned, it was too late to even call her. But come morning, he would drive to Claxton and they would talk and—

"Any reason you're out here alone, W?"

He turned to York. "Needed a breath of fresh air."

"Well, you're needed back inside."

Winston raised a brow. "Why?"

"A newcomer to the party, a woman who's a real looker. Virgil and Zion, not to mention those bad news Steele brothers, are all over her. Not giving her breathing room and making passes right and left."

"And just what do you want me to do about it?"

"Take her off their hands. They're crowding her and I think she's someone you'd want to spend time with."

Winston turned away and looked off in the distance. "You're wrong." He turned back to York. "Although it almost killed me to do so, I leveled with you, man, about something I needed to admit. I knew either you, X or U would understand."

"I did. I understood more than you know," York said in a low tone, placing his hands in his pockets and looking at Winston with an intense expression on his face.

Winston's visage darkened. "No, I don't think you did. If you had, then you wouldn't be trying to shove another woman my way this soon," he said in a curt tone, his anger rising.

York squared his shoulders. "Like I said, I understood more than you know…which is why the woman was invited when I ran into her earlier today."

York paused a second then added, "And did I happen to mention her name is Ainsley? Ainsley St. James?"

The glass of wine Winston brought up to his lips froze in its path. "Ainsley? *My* Ainsley?" he asked in an incredulous tone.

York shrugged. "It's the same woman whose picture I saw on your refrigerator when you asked me to get out the lemonade that day. I ran into her at a restaurant in Manhattan today and invited her to the party. As far as her being *your* Ainsley, the jury is still out on that, especially since V and Z, along with the brothers Tyson, Mercury and Gannon Steele are in there vying for her attention."

Before York could finished what he was saying Winston shoved the wine glass in his hand and walked swiftly toward the French doors.

* * *

"And you've never been to Phoenix?" the man who'd been introduced as Tyson Steele was asking her.

Ainsley shook her head smiling. He was handsome as sin. In fact all five men who were shamelessly flirting with her were. But as far as she was concerned, none had anything on the one man who held her heart. Uriel said he'd headed to the balcony. Had he seen her and gone out there to avoid her? "That's right. I've never been to Phoenix," she said, taking another sip of her wine.

"Then we need to invite you out for a visit," Tyson's brother Mercury suggested, his gaze roaming her up and down.

"And I think you should stay right here on the East Coast," Virgil interjected, moving closer to her.

Ainsley's heartbeat kicked up a notch, not from Virgil's movement, but from the man she saw coming through the French doors off the balcony. He glanced over at her. The moment their eyes connected, she was swamped by every emotion she'd felt when she'd seen him that first night in Hilton Head. But the deep brown eyes holding hers were intense and unreadable. Was he or wasn't he glad to see her? She desperately needed some sort of sign.

He then gave her one when his mouth curved in a smile. Releasing a deep sigh of relief, she couldn't help but smile back. And then he began walking toward her with the same sense of purpose he'd had that first night at the Sparrow.

At the same time, of their own accord, her feet began moving in his direction. "Ainsley? Where are you going?" one of the men asked, but she couldn't respond. She kept walking toward the one man she'd fallen head over heels in love with, although he didn't have a clue.

Moments later he was there and they stood facing each

other. Neither said anything as if they were deer caught in the headlights of each other's gazes. But she felt it, the sexual chemistry they seemed to generate so easily between them. And she didn't have to glance around to know others were watching them, probably feeling it, as well. But he didn't care that they were the center of attention and neither did she.

What he did next proved that point.

"I miss you so damn much," he whispered before pulling her into his arms and taking her mouth right then and there. Immediately she felt her beating heart pressed against his chest and moaned when his tongue touched hers in one blazing kiss. He was glad to see her; she would say that with certainty.

"I hate to interrupt, but I take it you two know each other?"

She recognized Virgil Bougard's voice. Winston reluctantly broke off the kiss, and smoothly wrapped his arms around her waist, bringing her closer to his side. He eyed the five men who'd been holding her attention since she had arrived. "Yes, we know each other and let me go on record here and now by stating that she's mine."

A whisper of surprise escaped Ainsley's lips at the same time a look of total shock appeared on the faces of all five men. "You're actually placing your personal stamp on a woman?" Virgil asked in disbelief, while Mercury Steele reached out to touch Winston's forehead to see if perhaps he was running a fever.

Winston waved off Mercury's reach before he reached up to stroke the side of Ainsley's cheek tenderly. "Yes, that's exactly what I'm doing," he said holding her gaze.

Virgil frowned. "How did this happen?" he asked in a rough tone.

Winston glanced back at Virgil. "Wasn't looking. Didn't want it. But it happened. And I don't regret it did." Returning his gaze to Ainsley, he said, "Come, let's leave."

"She arrived less than fifteen minutes ago," Tyson said frowning.

"Which means she shared all of your company fifteen minutes too long." He then turned to Ainsley. "We'll go find York and Darcy, congratulate them on their first anniversary and then we're out of here."

"W, you're out of the club," Virgil said in a not-too-happy tone.

He glanced over at him. "I know."

"Winston…"

He always enjoyed hearing his name off her lips and tonight was no exception. After bidding good-night to York and Darcy, he hadn't wasted any time getting Ainsley to the Marriott Marquis in Times Square.

In the privacy of his hotel room, he admitted things to her that he'd wished he'd confessed before. In the cab ride over, she had explained why she hadn't taken the position of mayor and he'd told her why he hadn't stopped her from leaving that day.

And at present they were locked in a sensuous embrace making love. As soon as they closed the door behind them, they had begun tearing off each other's clothes and tumbled onto the bed.

And now he was sliding his body over her parted thighs, while cupping her face with his hands and staring down hard at her. And just to think that at one time he'd been convinced no woman could fill him with this many emotions. No woman could make him want to move heaven and earth for her.

He lowered his head and whispered against her wet lips words he figured he would never again say to a woman. "I love you."

"Oh, Winston, I love you, too. So much," she said, wrapping her arms around his neck and tightening her hold. He opened his mouth over hers at the same time he slid between her moist womanly folds, lifting her hips to go deep into her slick heat, all the way to the hilt.

And then he began moving in and out while his hands cupped her bottom low so that his fingers skimmed her inner thighs. He pulled his mouth and his hands away and she moaned out his name as he continued to ride her hard.

Tunneling his fingers through her hair, he held her gaze, knowing this was the woman that was meant to be his, and she was, and he wouldn't let her go. He would admit the thought of a long-distance romance scared the hell out of him, but he would do it if it came to that. But he'd learned his lesson never to assume that he knew what she wanted. He had been wrong the last time, which meant that maybe, just possibly, she would consider moving to Australia with him.

He lifted his head, arched his back and bucked at the straining of his muscles when he felt his entire body explode. "Ainsley!"

She cried out his name as somehow she opened her legs more and took him in even deeper. He looked down at her, saw her closed eyes and whispered, "Look at me, baby. I want you to look at me and feel the love. I love you and I need you."

She opened her eyes and locked her gaze with his when another explosion hit them both. Never had he desired a woman so much. Loved one to such a degree that he trembled all over.

A short while later with their naked limbs entwined, he held her in his arms as her head rested on his chest. "I'm leaving the country for a while."

Ainsley lifted her head to stare at him, certain he could see all the questions in her gaze.

"I've been given the opportunity to work in Australia at the Great Barrier Reef."

"To do more studies on the turtles?" she asked.

"Yes."

She leaned up as a smile touched her lips, knowing how much he wanted that. "Oh, Winston, that's great."

"Yes, but I don't want to leave you behind."

She pulled herself up. "Then don't. Take me with you."

His gaze widened. "You'd go? Leave your work here and travel with me there? It will be for three years."

"I don't care if it will be for thirty years. I can write articles from anywhere and I don't need that plush office after all. I want to be with you."

He smiled. "And I want to be with you." He pulled her back down in his arms. "You know what that means, right?"

She had an idea but wanted him to tell her. "What does it mean?"

"That I want you to be Mrs. Winston Coltrane."

She chuckled. "Is that a proposal?"

"You bet it is. If you prefer the more traditional on-your-knees kind of proposal, I can do that, as well."

She shook her head. "No, all I want is your undying love as you'll have mine."

"Baby, you got it." He then eased her up closer over his body, so his mouth could reach hers. "I love you, Ainsley," he whispered against her moist lips.

"And I love you, too."

And he captured her mouth and kissed her with a hunger

he felt all through his body. This love was meant to be. He had joined the ranks of totally whipped men and he wouldn't have it any other way.

Epilogue

The bright sun beamed down on the couple as they stood before the minister being joined as man and wife.

They were on Barrett Shores on this glorious day in June, in an outdoor wedding with a beautiful view of the ocean in front of them. "I now pronounce you man and wife. Winston, you may kiss your bride."

Ainsley turned and Winston lifted the veil from her face and leaned in to claim her lips. She knew his kiss would be powerful, shake her to the core and probably be too lusty for the two-hundred guests assembled oceanside.

He finally released her mouth, grinned over at his five godbrothers and gave each a thumbs-up...even Virgil and Zion. They weren't happy that the Bachelors in Demand Club had dwindled from six members down to two, but they were happy for Winston and she appreciated that. She was counting on them finding their true love like she and Winston had. After all, she was convinced that everyone had a soul mate.

Holding hands she and Winston turned to face their guests as the minister said, "Ladies and gentlemen, I present to you Mr. and Mrs. Winston Coltrane."

She heard the clapping, cheers, whistles and catcalls. But what she would remember most was Winston pulling her back into his arms and kissing her again. Later tonight before they left for their honeymoon in Ireland, she intended to dance for her husband. She intended to strip for him, as well. But what she really intended to do was be his mate for life.

She gasped when be broke off the kiss and swung her up into his arms to stride away from the beachside wedding party. She was happy, overjoyed and elated with how the day had turned out and was ready to start a new life with the man she loved.

The bachelor that was unclaimed no more.

* * * * *

New York Times **Bestselling Author**

BRENDA JACKSON

High-powered lawyer Brandon Washington knew how
to win. He had to be ruthless, cutthroat and, for his
latest case, irresistible. His biggest client, the family of
the late hotel magnate John Garrison, had sent Brandon
under an assumed name to the Bahamas to track down
their newly discovered half sister. He would find her,
charm her and uncover all her secrets.

But as soon as Brandon met the beautiful heiress, the
lines began to blur. Between the truth and the lies.
Between her secrets and his. Between his ambition…and
a chance to be loved. And as a storm gathered over the
Caribbean, Brandon knew the reckoning was coming.
And this time, winning could be the last thing he wanted.

STRANDED WITH THE TEMPTING STRANGER

Available February 26 wherever books are sold!

Plus, ENJOY the bonus story *The Executive's Surprise Baby*
by *USA TODAY* **bestselling author Catherine Mann,**
included in this 2-in-1 volume!

www.Harlequin.com

NYTBJ0313

REQUEST YOUR FREE BOOKS!

2 FREE NOVELS PLUS 2 FREE GIFTS!

KIMANI™ ROMANCE

Love's ultimate destination!

YES! Please send me 2 FREE Kimani™ Romance novels and my 2 FREE gifts (gifts are worth about $10). After receiving them, if I don't wish to receive any more books, I can return the shipping statement marked "cancel." If I don't cancel, I will receive 4 brand-new novels every month and be billed just $4.94 per book in the U.S. or $5.49 per book in Canada. That's a savings of at least 21% off the cover price. It's quite a bargain! Shipping and handling is just 50¢ per book in the U.S. and 75¢ per book in Canada.* I understand that accepting the 2 free books and gifts places me under no obligation to buy anything. I can always return a shipment and cancel at any time. Even if I never buy another book, the two free books and gifts are mine to keep forever.

168/368 XDN FVUK

Name _____ (PLEASE PRINT)

Address _____ Apt. #

City _____ State/Prov. _____ Zip/Postal Code

Signature (if under 18, a parent or guardian must sign)

Mail to the Harlequin® Reader Service:
IN U.S.A.: P.O. Box 1867, Buffalo, NY 14240-1867
IN CANADA: P.O. Box 609, Fort Erie, Ontario L2A 5X3

Want to try two free books from another line?
Call 1-800-873-8635 or visit www.ReaderService.com.

* Terms and prices subject to change without notice. Prices do not include applicable taxes. Sales tax applicable in N.Y. Canadian residents will be charged applicable taxes. Offer not valid in Quebec. This offer is limited to one order per household. Not valid for current subscribers to Kimani Romance books. All orders subject to credit approval. Credit or debit balances in a customer's account(s) may be offset by any other outstanding balance owed by or to the customer. Please allow 4 to 6 weeks for delivery. Offer available while quantities last.

Your Privacy—The Harlequin® Reader Service is committed to protecting your privacy. Our Privacy Policy is available online at www.ReaderService.com or upon request from the Harlequin Reader Service.

We make a portion of our mailing list available to reputable third parties that offer products we believe may interest you. If you prefer that we not exchange your name with third parties, or if you wish to clarify or modify your communication preferences, please visit us at www.ReaderService.com/consumerschoice or write to us at Harlequin Reader Service Preference Service, P.O. Box 9062, Buffalo, NY 14269. Include your complete name and address.

KROM13

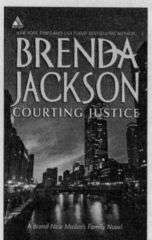

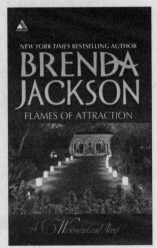